Mothers and Other Strangers

Mothers and Other Strangers

STORIES BY
BUDGE WILSON

Budge Wilson

Harcourt Brace & Company
San Diego   New York   London

Library of Congress Cataloging-in-Publication Data
Wilson, Budge.
Mothers and other strangers: stories/Budge Wilson.
p.   cm.
Contents: The listener—Loretta and Alexander—Elliot's
daughter—Just give me a little more time—Mrs. Macintosh—
The house on High Street—Birds, horses, and muffins—The
diary—The Courtship.
ISBN 0–15–200312–6
1. Short stories, Canadian. [1. Short stories.] I. Title.
PZ7.W69004Mo 1996
[Fic]—dc20 95–17579

Text set in Bembo
Designed by Judythe Sieck

First edition
F E D C B A

Printed in the United States of America

For my friend Jane Buss,
gratefully

Contents

The Listener

"WELL, IT'S MY OPINION, for what it's worth, that she's basically dumb. If you accept that fact, it explains everything." It was Sandra who was speaking. And of course we listened. One did not ignore Sandra. She was like her name, inside and out. Exotic. And a little overdone. The parents of 1928 had not often given their daughters names like Sandra.

When I first met her, it was 1945. The first-year class was full of Annes and Jeans and Marys, and when we met a Sandra or a Diana or an Ericka, we reacted with a mixture of disapproval and envy. But we noticed. And we remembered.

Sandra was dressed that day in a red angora sweater that was a bit too tight, a trace too red. Her lipstick was so dark, so wet, that if she had brushed against your white sweater accidentally, you would have had to throw it away. She had long, thick black hair, which fell over one eye in the fashion of the year. She also had strong opinions, no visible inhibitions, and a warm heart.

But Sandra's heart did not reach out lovingly to Jane. It was the end of initiation week, and we already knew more about one another than it was always comfortable to know. We had formed a small knot of four friends—an anomalous grouping, based on the occupancy of two double rooms that faced one another at the end of a narrow corridor in the university residence.

Barbara was speaking now, fixing Sandra with a bland stare behind her thick rimless glasses. "Whatever else she is," she stated quietly but firmly, with a stolid authority, "dumb she is not. I would stake my scholarship on it." Barbara had her own share of forceful judgments, but they were delivered with a rhetorical thud. You couldn't win the highest entrance scholarship to Dalhousie at age sixteen without a penetrating mind, but you could win it without flair. Barbara was loyal and honest and very intelligent indeed. She had a round, serene face, straight brown hair, which she did not bother to curl, and a small, neat, nicely built body. She wore a beige sweater with a Peter Pan collar and a brown pleated skirt. During the whole three years I knew her at college, I think she wore the same pair of tan-colored loafers.

We were walking home from the last football game of that busy week, along the cinder path above the bleachers, toward the pine woods to the east of the residence. The afternoon sun was already behind the trees, and the late September day was chilly. I hugged myself inside my brand new black blazer (piped with gold braid) and shivered. I assumed it was time for me to offer my verdict.

"Well," I said, kicking a stone ahead of me as I walked along, "she's certainly not your hundred percent typical freshette, and she's awfully *quiet,* but good grief, we don't all have to be exactly *alike.*" I looked at the two of them, and thought about the way neither of them fitted into any mold that I could recognize. "At least," I added, "you've got to admit that she's a good listener."

"Oh, a good *listener!*" Sandra threw her arms into the air. "We're all good *listeners.*" I wasn't so sure about that, but I was still struggling with my chronic shyness and said nothing. Sandra was continuing her speech, walking along the woods path with her hips swinging, her hair bouncing. She looks French, I thought; I wish I could be like that—free and open and so *physical.* How can she be all of those things when she's only seventeen? "It's all very well to be a good listener," retorted Sandra, "but she could once in a while *say* something. She gives

me the almighty creeps, and I still think she's dumb."
She swung along with her coltlike grace. "And if she *is*,"
she added, "I can maybe forgive her."

"Well," said Barbara, "she's not. So you can forget it."

Sandra turned abruptly to me. "OK, Ginny. What
about you? You're the one who has to room with her.
What do you *really* think? I mean *really*. Being a good
listener just isn't enough."

I swallowed, and tried to choose my words carefully.
I would be living with Jane for the next eight months,
and I didn't want to declare war in the first week. On
the other hand, I liked Sandra and Barbara and wanted
them to approve of me. I lacked their strong, indepen-
dent confidence, and I was also without their firm con-
victions. If I sounded wise and fair, it was simply because
I had no idea who I was or what I believed. "I think,"
I faltered, "that maybe we'd better wait a while before
we decide what makes her tick." I hoped this hadn't
sounded too bland, or worse still, too goody-goody.
"Maybe she's shy," I added, "like me."

With the end of introductory week, real academic life
began, and often we were too busy to gossip. Sandra,
who was as well endowed intellectually as she was phys-

ically, saved her work for the nights before essays were due and for the month that preceded exams. She already had a lineup of admirers, and when she was not out on the town with one or another of them (i.e., at the movies, at the Friday dance, or in the soda shop), she seemed to live in the phone booth. When the second-floor phone rang and the voice yelled, "Second Wing!" down the hollow stairwell, we could be pretty sure that the call was for Sandra. She had come to Dalhousie to find a boyfriend, and she was working hard on the project. On her calendar, she stuck red stars to indicate the significance of the function or the man of that day. Little green circular stickers denoted failed operations. An occasional boy merited two stars. But she was not going to settle for anything less than a four-star guy.

Barbara was busy and preoccupied in her own way, too. She knew exactly why she had come to college, and by the end of her second week, she had formed a pattern to her life that seldom varied. She worked. The library was to Barbara what the dance floor was to Sandra. It was her spiritual center and her heart's home. It was also her path to success, and she walked that path without a glance to the right or to the left. With seven brothers and sisters and a blue-collar father, she had a compelling need to keep her scholarship for six straight years. Her more frivolous inclinations she kept well hidden. Probably only our small clique at the end of the corridor was aware that she loved comic books, that she licked all-day suckers while she worked on essays, that she had a crush on Gregory Peck.

I was the typical coed of that time, and I certainly do not say this boastfully. I had no idea what I wanted to do with my life, and I was attending Dalhousie simply because my parents had sent me. I was thrilled by the possibilities that college life offered, and I felt that if I could ever conquer my paralyzing shyness, the place would be able to deliver fun, guys, social adventures, and infinite diversions—on the *Gazette* staff, on the basketball floor, on campus executives. I passed courses with a minimum of effort and found their content interesting and often exciting. However, I fell in love during the second week of January in my first year, and from then on, I seesawed back and forth between agony and bliss; all other matters took a backseat to my need and compounding failure to capture and keep Tony O'Brien for my very own. I did not possess the psychic energy required for solving the mystery of Jane.

After a while I think we all stopped trying to understand the sources of Jane's peculiarities. We were too involved with our own lives to care. She was there.

She had hot chocolate with us at 9:00 P.M. during the break from Quiet Hours. She accompanied us on our trips to Joe's, where, for a ten-cent cup of coffee, we occupied a whole booth for up to two hours. She sat and listened while Sandra assessed her boyfriends, while Barbara planned her career, while I lamented my inability to wheedle even one invitation out of Tony, or while I raptured over the fact that he had said hello to me that afternoon.

When I think back to the Jane of those days, I see a tiny figure with a cap of curly hair and enormous eyes. She could have been cute, but something in her expression or in herself prevented it. She hardly ever smiled. And when she did, it was just a stretching of the mouth, communicating nothing of warmth or pleasure. If you told her of your worries or miseries, however, she would sit with her head a little to one side, and look you straight in the eye, clucking sympathetically.

I think Jane ceased to be a real person to us. She never offered details of her own life or aspirations, nor did she gossip about the other girls. She didn't even discuss her courses. She simply became the repository of our confidences—safe, silent. She wore black baggy slacks over her skinny haunches and a loose black sweater over her flat chest. A pair of round steel-rimmed glasses emphasized her large, penetrating eyes. As the years went by, most of her courses were in English and psychology, and in spite of Sandra's early predictions, her marks were good. She spent long hours alone in our room, with the door shut.

I don't know why we ever complained about Jane at that time. She was very useful to all of us. Use is the key word. We *used* her. When Sandra was out searching for the four-star man, when Barbara was holed up in the library, it was to Jane that I went when I wanted to complain about a demanding professor or to question the meaning of an essay topic, or to discuss the frustrations of my unrequited love for Tony O'Brien. She always had time to listen; she never interrupted. I became very grateful for that slightly inclined head, those interested and quietly sympathetic eyes, her monosyllabic expressions of encouragement or pity. "Sad!" she would murmur or "Wow!" or one of many variations of "Oh." That was enough for me, and gradually it became enough for all of us.

I first met Tony O'Brien at a Drama Club party, although *met* is certainly a loose definition of what took place. I was an invisible alto in the chorus, and he was working as chief designer on the set. Incredible though it seemed to me when I saw him that night, I had never noticed him before. He had a rugged and irregular face, with a mop of unruly dark blond hair. He was almost skinny and very tall, but his long arms and legs moved with coordination and confidence. He was beautiful. He looked at me across a roomful of faces and noise, with what I was convinced was a come-hither look. Thus I described it to Jane when I woke her up at 1:30 A.M. to announce the onset of my emotional bondage. When I had felt Tony's gaze embracing me, I was in the process of eating a hot dog. I remember with a burning clarity that my mouth was open to receive my first bite and that my hand was poised to deliver it.

Frozen like Lot's wife, I stood there with my mouth wide open, the hot dog in midflight. Only when I started to feel the mustard dribbling down my arm did I move. By then the mustard was landing on my shoes in large yellow blobs. At which point, to my overwhelming embarrassment, Tony threw back his marvelous head and roared with laughter. When he stopped laughing and delivered to me his wide, warm smile, I was in no mood to receive it. Fiery hot with the depth of shame that only a shy person can feel, I threw the offending wiener into a nearby split-leaf philodendron, and turned my back upon that radiant and welcoming face. Striking up a spirited conversation with a pimply youth called Avery, whom I had never spoken to before, I spent the rest of the evening avoiding any visual contact with the laughing stranger. This apparently insignificant half hour was to set the pattern for my dealings with both Tony and Avery for the next two and a half years. Avery, who was receiving the rapt attention of a pretty girl for perhaps the first time in his seventeen-year-old life, fell in love with me—instantly, and more or less permanently—remaining a problem to me during all my years at Dalhousie. Eventually, three years later, in frustration and despair, he would move to British Columbia. He told me he hoped that distance might offer some healing for his bruised, neglected heart. I felt only relief when he went. It never crossed my mind that he was suffering as acutely as I was, and from the same disease.

Love was a grim game at that time, in the late '40s. It was destructive and it was intense; it could also be as thrilling and romantic as the movies of that time. But it was a game, nonetheless. Not until the free and open '60s did young men and women dare to look at one another as people. In my time, every man we talked to, however briefly, tended to be regarded as a potential "date"—to be spurned or encouraged, avoided or seduced. And those dates merited special clothes, special behavior, special responses. We were terrible women in those days. We were cruel to the unloved and unwanted; we picked them up and dropped them like Kleenex or candy bar wrappers. By the same token, we were the helpless victims of philanderers and of those who did not know that we were alive. And we had few weapons with which to play our deadly game; what's more, the rules were so numerous and stringent that it was almost impossible to win. Only the Sandras of that world could hope to succeed in spite of the constricting conventions of the time. With half the male world flocking to her doorstep, it might still be hard for her to find the perfect man. It might take time. But ultimately, all she had to do was choose.

When I returned that night and told Jane that I had met my fate and my future, she listened with her usual quiet concern. It was the first of many outpourings on my part, because the love game for me was so difficult and disheartening. It was 1946, and I could not simply march up to Tony and say, "Hey, I think you look wonderful, and I have forgiven you for laughing at my open mouth and at the mustard rolling down my arm. Please call me. Let's get to know one another." If you were not *asked* out, you didn't *go* out. Waiting is one of the most savage memories for a woman who was a shy girl during those years. She waited for a smile, a greeting, a sign that someone was attracted. Most of all, she waited for the phone to ring. Even if it did ring with invitations from other men, even if the girl accepted those offers, even if in the eyes of her world she was busy and popular, she was still waiting, still on hold, until such time as the right person surfaced with the right overture, the right proposal.

And so it was with me. I was blond and pretty, with long legs and clear skin; I also had a good brain, athletic ability, and no self-confidence. But the blond good looks brought me invitations to most of the weekly dances and to more movies than I have ever seen since that time. I hid my shyness behind a smiling exterior, and channeled my frustrations into campus organizations, into the gymnasium, into the Drama Club. I also studied for my courses—more than Sandra, less than Barbara.

I had a mediocre voice and no dramatic talent, but I clung to the Drama Club, knowing that this was where I would be free to admire the chief set designer and painter. And I was right. Tony was always there. Occasionally he would speak to me. At such moments, my heart would pound so dangerously and my breath desert me so utterly that I was unable to act normally, whatever that meant. I was full of laughter with the rest of the world. Around Tony, I was reduced to a stupefied silence

or to a conversation that would have bored a kindergar-
tener. Sometimes I would catch him looking at me with
his piercing look. I would bat my eyelashes at him in
reply and smile what I hoped was a provocative smile.
But our person-to-person encounters always fizzled out.

I don't know how I would have coped with such a
split existence without Jane. She heard all, never judged,
accepted my confidences without comment or cen-
sure—or even advice. And because I had that outlet for
my pain, I had the strength to continue my futile pursuit
of Tony O'Brien and to act, when in the presence of the
rest of the Dalhousie population, as though everything
was perfect in this best of all possible worlds.

Graduation was a sad day for me. I felt no pride upon
receiving my diploma. It had been easy to get, and I
could see no great cause for rejoicing. All I could think
of that day, as I flipped my blond hair over the edge of
my hood and prepared to line up for the procession, was
that this was the end of the road. I was about to step out
into a life that contained no Drama Club. There would
be no chance meetings with Tony at the back door of
the gym, no accidental encounters backstage. The world
was big out there, and I knew it. I would never again be
able to admire Tony—daily—from the other side of the
soda shop, as he drank his Coke with his pals. I confided

my feelings to Jane, who was beside me in the procession. And I realized with an extra stab of pain that I would not even have my mother-confessor in the years ahead of me. She was leaving the following week for Toronto, to take a summer job in a publishing house, before starting an M.A. in English at the University of Toronto. Barbara was going on to law school in the fall; and Sandra was planning her wedding in September to the four-star man whom she had met two months earlier, on Munro Day—what other schools called Founder's Day. I had a summer job emptying wastebaskets and running errands at the *Halifax Chronicle,* and I didn't anticipate my future with enthusiasm. Tony would be leaving in the autumn for the Ontario College of Art.

Five years later, Sandra and Barbara and I were still living in Halifax. Sandra was juggling a three-year-old son, twin baby girls, and a successful marriage. Barbara was working for a prestigious law firm and doing legwork for the Liberal Party. Basically, neither had changed. Sandra, harassed by three children under three, still managed to look seductive and vibrant as she moved from clothesline to roasting pan to ironing board to diaper bucket. Barbara had achieved one large goal, but had her sights on a future judgeship or a career in politics. Clad in beige suits with simple brown blouses, she still went about her business with unruffled efficiency. After my years at college, I was a reporter on the *Chronicle* now, enjoying a growing confidence in my own worth, taking pleasure in a social life that kept me busy and entertained. The memory of Tony O'Brien had dimmed somewhat, but I had found no one else with whom I was interested in sharing my life.

In the spring of that year, the *Halifax Chronicle* carried a review of a new book published by Claxton Press, one of Canada's most prominent publishing houses. The review read: "This is a first novel by a promising young writer, who could be Canada's answer to Mary McCarthy. The book is hilarious but penetrating; it entertains, but with the strong ring of truth. If you've ever attended a university or lived in a large residence, don't miss this book. You'll meet yourself on every page."

The book had been written by Jane.

Of course, we all rushed out to buy it. We didn't buy one copy and lend it around. No one could wait that long. We all contributed to her royalties.

On the first page of the book I read the usual blurb about the characters: ". . . no resemblance," it read, "to any persons living or dead." Then I turned to page one and started to read the story of four girls who lived together for three years at college in Alberta. One of the four girls was the narrator and had no real color or form. The others were called Angela, Helen, and Julie. They were Sandra, Barbara, and me.

It was all there, everything. The past came speeding back with an impact that was grotesque. It was as though the years between had not existed. Even as I read each succeeding page with increasing horror, a grudging part of me admitted that the book was brilliantly written, a masterpiece of humor and clarity and even of poignancy.

"And why," stormed Sandra from the other end of the phone line that afternoon, "would it not be brilliantly written? She didn't have to exercise her horrid little brain, her bizarre imagination, for one single second. We provided her with every line of her material. All she had to do was string it together like beads." Sandra had called me at the end of Chapter Two. She had already encountered herself in her red angora sweater, collecting men like postage stamps, searching avidly for the four-star man. "I'd better go," she said. "I'm scared to death to read another word, but I've got to finish it today. Mother has taken the kids for twenty-four hours, and I may never get a chance like this again. I could *die!* I could *kill* her! And I know exactly what Barbara's going to say." She hung up without saying good-bye.

And Barbara, true to form, said it, when she called an hour later. "I told you she wasn't dumb," she said, with a sad chuckle. "I've just finished it, and I can tell you this: that blotter of a mind of hers absorbed every single peculiarity, the smallest tic, all the intricate aspects of personality or behavior that any of us ever exhibited." Her perpetually calm voice was rising in a manner that was new to my ears. "Ginny!" she said, words cracking, "even the all-day suckers are there! Who is ever going to vote for a Liberal candidate who eats suckers when she works—and who was head over heels in love with Gregory Peck? Or who was devoted to *comic books?*" She paused, and then went on. "I'd sue," she said, "for all of us—and *free*—except that then the whole world would know who was walking around in that book." There was another pause. "Our only hope," she said quietly, very solemnly, "is to act as though this novel had never been written." Then she laughed shakily. "I'm going out this afternoon to buy a red dress. I've just spent eight hours with *Helen,* and she wore a beige sweater the entire time. And strike me dead if I ever wear a pair of loafers again. Ginny. It's not fair. I don't want to change, even to protect myself. I *like* beige." She sighed. "Bye, Ginny," she said.

Like Barbara, I had read the whole book. I sat there

in my little bachelor apartment and looked around me. I had been so proud of it. It had been a symbol to me of my new independence, my growing respect for myself as a freestanding individual, as a person of value, as someone with a *mind*. Suddenly, the little living room looked pathetic to me, the brave attempt of a disappointed person to come to terms with an inadequate life. The white walls. The lone lithograph, framed in black. The spartan teak table with its woven gray placemats. Everything in bleak good taste. No color. Sandra and Barbara, I noted, were angry. Barbara was even uneasy, fearful for her career. But no one, I thought, as I stared out the window, is as *hurt* as I am.

I felt exhausted, as though I never again wanted to rise from my chair. For one awful ironic moment, I longed for Jane's presence, so that I could confide my pain to her. "The betrayal of trust," I said aloud, and grieved for a dead friendship, buried without honor. But my chief lament was for the unmasking of my real personality and of my hopeless love for Tony O'Brien. For he, too, of course, was in the book—bright eyes shining, smiling his welcome, leaving me to wait by the silent telephone. Sandra had been depicted as flashy, frivolous, clever, and lazy, the pursued and the pursuing, successful in her quest for the four-star man. Barbara had been shown to be quiet, fiercely ambitious, drab in appearance, with a brilliant mind. And a person who had reached her first goal with much success and no regrets. There were no surprises here, and no insults capable of inflicting a mortal wound.

But for me, the book meant much, much more. I had been living a lie for so long that even I had come to believe that it was true. Tossing my blond hair, I had sailed through three years of university, presenting myself as being full of confidence and fun, trailing a string of small successes. But too many scenes in Jane's book described the tears in my eyes. Now, all my Dalhousie friends—who would certainly read the book hungrily from cover to cover—would know that I really had been and probably still was scared, dependent, socially inept, and the person who had loved Tony O'Brien with a love that was futile and public and humiliating.

One week later, my boss on the *Chronicle* called me over to his desk. "I have an assignment for you," he said. "It's not exactly in your field, but we're short-staffed this week, and you're just going to have to do it."

"Sure," I said. "Anything. Anything is fine." A fire, a break-in, a City Council scandal—something absorbing enough to take my mind off that damn novel.

"It's that new book that everyone's suddenly talking about. You may have read Harriet's review of it last week. It became a runaway best-seller within a month of publication. And the writer's a local girl."

I stood there, not breathing.

"Well," he went on, "she's in town. A big blue-blood book club is giving a giant reception today in her honor. Cover it. Drop a few big names. In Halifax you can always count on a few admirals or cabinet members or Supreme Court wives. Jazz it up. Make it a social piece, but with a difference."

"What difference?" I managed to ask.

"Not just social," he said. "Literary. Egghead. Something that will appeal to the university brass. Get an interview with the woman."

"Please," I breathed.

"Please what?" he asked, as he rose to attend an editorial meeting.

"Please, no," I begged. I almost added, "I knew her once, and she is my deadly enemy," but remembered in time that from now on, I was supposed to act as though I had never laid eyes on her.

He was not amused. "Don't be silly, Ginny," he barked. "You've only had this job for a year, and I'm afraid you don't have any choice about this kind of thing. Twelve months ago you were sharpening pencils."

Slap. "You're right, Mr. Cameron," I said, ever pliant, always the yes-woman. Go do a story on the realities of hanging. Put your head in a noose and let the rope tighten. Then, if breath remains, come back here and write a brilliant piece for, say, page seven. "You're absolutely right," I heard myself repeating. "What are the details?"

He gave them to me. "Five to seven-thirty P.M. The Council of Women building on Young Avenue. Cocktails. Dress like you belong there. Keep your press card in your handbag unless asked to show it. Melt into the crowd. Keep your ears open."

"Yes, Mr. Cameron."

I arrived at 163 Young Avenue at six-fifteen, fashionably late, but early enough to observe every single guest. I was hoping for a mob to get lost in. I got it. I was wearing a black cocktail dress with a wide swirling skirt, held out by the fullest crinoline I could find. My neckline plunged, and my blond hair and milky skin looked pale and pure against the material of the dress. Believe it or not, that's the kind of thing you wore to a cocktail party in those days. Stealing a look at myself in a full-length mirror, I was pleased. "You look fantastic," I whispered to my reflection. "This, too, shall pass," I added, without conviction. I wished that I were wearing a pair of dark glasses.

The enormous rooms were full of noisy people, screaming their cocktail party talk, pressing close to hear one another. Willing myself to avoid thinking about the pending interview, I made mental notes of newsworthy people on the guest list. After half an hour, I made a discreet trip to the rest room to write the information on a pad I always carried with me. Six university professors. Four judges' wives, one judge. Three local authors and one cabinet minister. A beer baron. Lots of military and naval wives. Assorted hangers-on. The top drawer of the town. Clearly this book had made its mark. My stomach lurched.

Upon returning to the largest room, a break in the crowd allowed me to witness a scene in the exact center of the floor. There she was, oddly the same and yet profoundly changed. The baggy sweater and pants had given way to a loose black dress, deceptively simple, undeniably elegant. It was made of a soft wool that fell gracefully and was nipped in at her tiny waist by a wide black belt with a large gold buckle. She wore a long, thin gold chain and no other jewelry. I was already regretting my crinoline, my bare chest. Instead of her close-cropped curls, her hair was worn in a premature Afro. Much later, the style would become fashionable. At that time, it was arresting, courageous. It told the onlookers that although she was dressed with a subdued taste that could satisfy the haughtiest critic on Young Avenue, she could also be daring, artistic—her own confident, talented self.

I took in all of this at a glance, and then made myself watch what was taking place on that little island in the middle of the room. She was not talking. Her head was slightly bent, and she was listening carefully to the spirited conversation of one of the guests. Her eyes, intent behind her new fashionable glasses, never wandered from her companion's face. The guest was leaning close to her, as though speaking quietly, delivering up a secret. Oh, be careful, be careful, my heart cried out to that woman. If you're telling about your failed marriage, your wicked uncle, your past sins, stop before it's too late. Worse still, if you're a rising young writer discussing your work, keep your plots to yourself, lest you discover them on someone else's pages. Beware, beware.

Finally I took two slow deep breaths and did what I had to do. As the other guest moved off, I approached Jane and stood in front of her, holding my martini in what I prayed was a nonchalant manner. I did not smile. "Hello, Jane," I said. "I'm from the *Halifax Chronicle*. I'd like an interview."

A faint flicker of what I like to think was alarm moved across her face. Then she smiled her cold nonsmile and said, "Ginny! How nice. But surely not an interview. Here?"

"Yes," I said. "Here. Tell me about your life, your work. Tell me," I could not resist adding, "how you dream up your wonderful plots."

"Oh no," she protested, cocking her head sideways, in readiness. "I'm bored with me. Tell me all about yourself."

I looked her full in the face for a moment before I said, "No thank you," and turned and walked away. If I was to lose my job over this, fine. Some things, I discovered, just cost too much.

As I reached the opposite side of the room, I felt a hand on my shoulder. "You did that very well indeed," said the voice behind the hand. "I'm proud to know you." I didn't have to turn around to know who it was. His voice was as memorable as his face, as his laughter. I took another deep breath and faced him.

"Hello, Tony," I said. Jane had so irretrievably embarrassed me, and the part of my life with Tony had been so irrevocably damaged by her, that my shame had a kind of stillness to it that was releasing for me. There was no need to flutter and panic about what I would say to him. A certain peace evolves from the cessation of hope. "It's nice to see you again," I said. I looked at him and knew that my feeling for him was as fresh as it had been six years ago. "What on earth brings you to this amazing event?" I asked.

He pointed to an enormous camera sitting on a nearby table. "Here from *Maclean's*," he said. "To get a few pictures. I freelance for them, and they sent me down from an assignment in Truro to take some shots. I have a dozen or more. She's listening in every one of them." He looked at me sharply for a long moment, and then he said, "Ginny, can we talk? Let's find a place to sit." We sat down on a loveseat—what irony, I thought—in the alcove where he had been standing.

"Maybe I'm sticking my neck out," he began. "Maybe you don't care for me anymore, like you did in the book. Or maybe she made that part up. But if I don't say this now, I never will." He passed his hand briefly across his eyes. "I never could figure you out," he continued. "Sometimes you'd look at me as though you were interested. I even thought you blushed once in a while. But when I'd speak to you, you'd close right up, leaving me feeling like a leper. My hopes kept rising and falling. I used to watch you. With everyone else, you laughed and talked and were so warm. I finally decided it must have all gone back to the hot dog and the mustard. Perhaps, I thought, this lady never forgave me for laughing. But Ginny. I wasn't laughing *at* you. I was laughing with delight. You looked so great. And so bewildered. But I guess that kind of thing is hard to understand if you're the one who's dripping mustard all over your feet." There was a moment when he seemed to be struggling for control. But suddenly his voice broke, and he started to laugh. He threw back his head and laughed and laughed, until the blue-haired ladies stared and the admiral frowned and studied his drink.

For a moment, I withdrew into myself. Then, suddenly, to my astonishment, I felt something crack and burst inside of me, and I heard myself laughing so hard that I had to put down my martini and cross my arms over my sore stomach. Jane interrupted her listening for a moment to glance over, and then to look again.

When he stopped laughing, Tony became very sober and just sat there looking at me. I looked at him, too, very calm, very caring. All the while, I was thinking: Ginny, if you can manage to make yourself do what you want to do, you will prove to yourself that you are not the wimp described in Jane's novel. You will show that your new confidence is real, that you're not afraid to take chances. You will make a lie of that book.

Then, in the presence of all that social crust, at that time of Puritan and rigid rules of behavior, surrounded by the brains and professional talent of the city, in full view of Jane's astonished eyes, I took Tony's face between my hands and kissed him long and tenderly upon the lips.

The next day, I was somewhat late arriving at the office. The deadline for copy was dangerously near as I approached Mr. Cameron's desk.

"Well?" This was both an inquiry and a statement.

"I've got your story," I said to him. "Guests of note. Descriptions of the decor, the food, the dress worn by the guest of honor. But . . ." I paused here to prepare him. "She refused to give me an interview."

He frowned. "Bad luck," he sighed. "Dammit!"

"And I refused her mine," I said quietly.

"Pardon?" He was puzzled. Probably he thought he had heard incorrectly.

"Oh, nothing," I replied. "But look. I got you a really stunning picture. Never mind how. But it's an exclusive."

He grabbed it. "Great guns!" he rasped. "It's an editor's dream. Get me your piece fast. And lookit. Maybe you observed enough to write a little tidbit about her personally. In the picture she seems to be listening very intently to that woman. Perhaps you could play up her listening ability."

"Why, yes, Mr. Cameron, I think I could do just

that." I paused before returning to my own desk. "Oh, and Mr. Cameron—thank you for the assignment. I really enjoyed it."

"That Ginny!" I heard him say to the sports editor, as I moved off. "I'll never understand what makes her tick."

Loretta and Alexander

LORETTA WAS LUMPY in what most people would have regarded as all the wrong places. Her stomach was large and visible, and a second bulge—firmer and of less bulk, but nonetheless there—was situated between her waist and her breasts. Her face was not ugly, but its features were not noticeably much of anything else, either. Her cheeks did not cave in like Katharine Hepburn's, but rather puffed out, like a young child's. But Loretta was not a young child. She was eighteen years of age.

However, Loretta did have a couple of enviable qualities—apart from her soul, which we are not considering here. It is true that few people reached far enough beyond her lumpiness to notice them, but they existed. Loretta had exquisite skin. And not just on her face. All over. Her hands—dimpled, fat—looked as though they were made of the finest of creamy porcelain. Her legs, although large, were as smooth as the petals of some rare and delicate flower. The skin on her face looked as though it were lit from within, and was of a fragile and subtle transparency.

Loretta's eyes, her second physical asset, were not unusually large, but they were a remarkable teal blue color, bordering on green. The whites were uncommonly white and dependably so. She'd been known to cry for twenty consecutive minutes, then emerge with those whites intact. And around these lovely eyes was a fringe of splendid dark lashes—long, thick—bearing no relation whatsoever to her sparse, unruly hair of indeterminate shade, with its meandering center part.

Loretta had brought her beautiful skin and her blue-green eyes and her unlovely body to Gray Cliff Campground. Markedly uncoordinated, she was struggling now to pitch her tent. She had come alone, because her closest companions were either married or else making merry with their boyfriends. But it was July, and she had wanted to go camping. Loretta lacked the willpower to stick to a healthy diet, but in most other areas of her life, her will was centered and firm. If she wanted to go camping, she would go, and she would arrive early enough in the day to get the site with the best view. Deep down, she knew that someone her size should never wear shorts. But it was hot, so she wore them. She did not defiantly thumb her nose at potential disapproval. She simply did not care. She was equipped with a peaceful and unassuming self-confidence. Even in her struggles with the tent, there was an air of quiet acceptance.

Two sites to the north, Alexander drove his small truck into a parking space and turned off the ignition. He had been to this campground before. He knew which was the best site. And he'd missed it again, just as he'd missed it every one of the nine other times he'd been here. He sighed, squinting through his thick glasses to assess the people who had beat him to that sensational view. But from this distance, even with those telescope glasses, he couldn't make out more than a dim form doing something with a tent. And you can't feel exasperated for very long with a dim form.

However, it was easy for him to feel annoyed with himself. If only he hadn't taken the time to put out the garbage; it hadn't been even marginally smelly, and there was nothing in there to poison the cat. But he hadn't been sure. And he hadn't needed to check the stove and the windows and the front door—*four times*. He closed his eyes against this apparently permanent form of neuroticism. Other people just closed their doors and left their houses. Not Alexander. He left his house time after time, returning repeatedly to check something and then something else. Could the cat get at the litter box? Had he left the basement door open so that she could reach it? Was the coffee pot unplugged? (Mind you, he hardly ever used that pot. Still—all the more reason to be uncertain as to whether or not it was unplugged.) Had he turned off all the faucets, particularly in the bathroom sink, where there was no overflow opening? Yes, he had. Were the matches safely stowed in closed containers? Yes, they were. Had he put the chain on the back door? Yes, he had. When he'd left the house for the last time, he'd kept his eyes on the driveway, not wanting to see his neighbors staring at him from behind their curtains, tsk-tsking.

Alexander sighed again as he lifted his pup tent out of the trunk. What was in that house, anyway, worth stealing or burning or losing? Just a pile of dreary furniture from his nervous (and dead) mother, and cupboards full of unused staples (cream of tartar, paprika, vanilla) as well as a large can of WD-40. What did people use those things for anyway? And his files.

His files! Alexander's hands paused in midair. He'd forgotten to bring his box of files. If there were a fire, all his poetry would go up in smoke. His mind raced through his precautions to avoid fire. Yes, he was *sure* he'd unplugged the electric kettle. (But *had* he?) And he really could remember checking the stove tops and oven, placing the flat of his hands (for good measure) on top of each burner. (Or had that been this morning, before work?)

Alexander swallowed carefully. Should he go back? Would his uncertainty spoil the whole weekend? Chewing his lip, he put up his little tent without enthusiasm, his hands working mechanically and skillfully through all the motions. Then, with the same casual grace, he unpacked his other needs. Over supper, he'd make up his mind whether or not to return for his files. It was only a twenty-minute drive. Still, he'd love to feel really settled in. A trip back to town was an intrusion upon his peace. What peace? He took a deep breath and let it out slowly. It was his mother's fault. She'd been a chronic door and stove checker, and she'd been given to frequent bouts of anxiety. Savagely, Alexander drove the can opener into a tin of corned beef, cursing his genes.

Alexander's dexterity as he set up his Coleman stove, assembled pots and pans and bags of food, was at variance with his appearance. Bony and slightly stooped, he had the look of someone who was destined to trip over cracks and get tangled up in his own feet. But no. With training, with eyes less myopic, with a shorter frame, he had it within him to be a great dancer. But life for Alexander was full of a lot of if-onlys. If only he were more handsome, less nervous, more practical, less absentminded, more confident, less hesitant. Then, oh *then,* things would be different.

However, Alexander could be happy in this place, even with the wrong view. Poems just dropped out of the sky into his lap when he was here; in Gray Cliff Campground he felt as though he were plugged into some sort of poetical hotline. Even as he hungrily attacked his canned peas, he could feel a poem coming over him. Reaching into his pocket for a pencil and paper, he groaned aloud. Empty. It was conceivable that he might be able to cope with the absence of his file box. Without paper and pencil, the weekend was impossible.

In a state of mind bordering on panic, Alexander searched through the truck for pen, pencil, paper of any kind. Nothing. The world, it seemed, was composed of plastic. There were enough plastic bags stuffed under his seat to accommodate a novel, but even if he'd had something to write with, he couldn't have written a poem on *them.* And there was not a single paper bag in sight, nor envelope, nor even a stray used grocery list. He looked at the sites to the right and to the left of him, but the tenants had gone—to swim, to dine, to drive, to do anything except stay put, the thing that Alexander was so longing to do. He would approach the owners of the spectacular view. Maybe they would have a few sheets of paper they could spare and perhaps a stubby pencil they would be willing to lend.

As Alexander approached Site 15 (he knew the number by heart; had he not, after all, set up the number, the location, as a sort of cosmic and apparently unobtainable goal for himself?), he was no wiser about its tenancy. The large khaki tent was in a heap on the ground, and judging from the visible movement, at least one of the occupants of the area was underneath it.

When he reached the site, he waited beside the heaving tent and coughed carefully. Then a hand appeared, followed by a head. Alexander did not see any other part of the head except the eyes. It was as though a disembodied pair of eyes had appeared out of a khaki background. Marveling at the color, the profusion of lashes, he forgot for a moment why he had come.

"Hi," said Loretta, voice cheerful. "Looking for someone?"

"Yes," he said. "I mean, no. I'm looking for some-*thing*. But I see you're busy. I'm sorry to have disturbed you. What a beautiful view."

"That's OK," said Loretta. "I was just putting up my

tent." She laughed, her voice throaty and languid. "Or trying to. I'm all thumbs. I can't put a nail in a wall without getting bruises on every single one of my fingers. What are you looking for? And yes, the view's great. That's why I hotfoot it out here the *minute* I'm through work on my summer job. To get it before some other clown beats me to it."

Alexander sighed yet again. "May I help you?" he said. "Paper and pencil."

"What?"

"Paper and pencil. That's what I'm looking for. I need something to write with. And on. I write poetry. May I help you?" he repeated.

She looked at him. Poetry! And he didn't look as though he could help anyone or anything. A towering composition of unrelated bones, she mused. This is someone who obviously could break a leg getting out of bed. Still, four awkward hands might be more effective than two. "Yes, thank you," she replied. "The tent's kind of big. It was my father's from the days before tents got simple."

He was already picking up the scattered tent pegs, sorting ropes, lifting the center pole. "Here," he said, "hold this," and she took the pole, blindly obedient to something new in him. Speechless, she watched him go from task to task, moving with unerring smoothness and accuracy. No change of position was excessive or inept. Every physical thing he did had a kind of easy rhythm that was a pleasure to watch. He should be accompanied by music, she thought.

"OK," he said. "You can leave that now. Stand here while I fix the guy ropes and hammer in the pegs." Bending down to work on the pegs, he found himself cheek to cheek, as it were, with her leg. Words, images, metaphors, attacked him, as he let his eyes wander to that leg again and again, between hammer blows. Soft. That was certainly the key word. A hill of freshly fallen snow. No. Wrong color. A virgin sand dune.

"What happens to it when you get some sun?" he asked, reaching for another peg.

"What happens to what? The tent?"

"No. Your skin." Then he realized what he had said, and blushed.

She did not blush. "It gets brown. Sort of like strong coffee. I never burn."

He shut his eyes and let himself visualize the tanning of that skin.

"How do you get here so fast after work?" he asked.

"Well," she said, "I just tear home, get my stuff, feed the cat, and leave. I drive over the speed limit," she added.

"Tell me about your leaving," he asked, brows

contracted. The tent was up now, and he was sitting on the ground, leaning against a tree, hugging his knees, watching her eyes.

"My what?"

"Your leaving. How do you leave?"

"Your house?"

"Yes."

"Oh. Well . . ." She paused. "I just go. You know . . . *leave*. Check the stove . . ."

"Aha!"

Loretta stared at him. "Aha?"

"Yes. Aha! You check the stove. How many times?"

"Once. Why?"

He frowned. "And lock the door," he said, voice bleak. "Once, I suppose."

"Yes. *Why?*"

"Forget it. It's just that if you're neurotic, you kind of hope that maybe everyone else is, too." He told her why it was always impossible for him to get to the campground in time to get the best view. Then he stopped. Foot in his mouth again. *She,* after all, had the best view.

"Never mind." She grinned. "It's not like you beat dogs or steal paper clips or anything."

"Wow!" he said. "Do you mind if I write that down?"

"On what?" She grinned again.

"Right!" His face was relaxing, his brows unknotting. "Do you have some paper?"

She did. He might have known she would. "May I?" he asked, and settled down in her lawn chair to write a poem. It had just descended on him in one chunk when she'd mentioned dogs and paper clips. He glanced up for a moment, and she was sitting beside him.

"Oh!" he said. "Two chairs. Has your boyfriend gone for water?"

"No," she replied. "But I always bring two chairs. Just in case."

After writing for a while, he looked up from his poem, contemplating her eyes and her astonishing skin.

"I just bet," he said, "that you know exactly what to do with cream of tartar and paprika and vanilla. And WD-40."

She felt a warm peace pass over her and then settle deep into her chest. "Yes," she said. "As a matter of fact, I do."

He watched her, smiling quietly. "Beautiful view you've got here," he said.

"Yes," she said. "Haven't we."

Just give Me a Little More Time

I FORGET FROM WEEK to week how hard these pews are. The architect, or perhaps the designer of ecclesiastical furniture, must have had no knowledge of human anatomy. There is no possible way to lean back, and when you sit up straight, the curve of the wood thrusts your head forward. We look like a congregation of hens and roosters.

How Dr. MacDougal does drone on. Sometimes I almost wish I were an Anglican, or better still a Catholic, so that I could lose myself in the ritual of the service. The United Church of Canada does little to rescue you when the minister lacks charisma. Earnest, oh yes. Always earnest. But one wonders how a doctorate of divinity could ever have come his way, although there was something in the church bulletin last month about his "unusual talent for scholarship." I sit here speculating as to his field of research. No doubt some area closely related to human experience—something timely and relevant, such as the varied uses of the verb *to be* in the Book of Genesis.

I do wish that husband of mine would stop sniffling. The anthem is rather well done this morning, and all that nasal activity gets in the way of my enjoyment of it. "Sheep May Safely Graze." That new choirmaster from Sydney seems to be attracting some really remarkable voices. I would dig Donald in the ribs with my elbow to signal him to stop or perhaps hand him a handkerchief, but Gillian is sitting between us. And the best thing to do with Gillian these days is to give her a wide berth. I feel as though she were strewn with land mines. Carefully scrutinize your route and you may be OK. But one false move, and *watch out*. Sweet sixteen, indeed.

Goodness—Helena Thompson's hat is straight out of the '40s. Someone must have told her that hats are *in* again, and she's simply gone upstairs to her attic and dug one out of an old trunk. Doesn't she realize that only Princess Diana can get away with absurd headgear? Come to think of it, though, Gillian could do it, with that arresting face, those cornflower blue eyes. But that bunch of velvet violets dribbling down over Helena's left ear is certainly impeding my spiritual contemplation of the Old Testament reading.

Hymns. How I do love them. Sometimes I think they're the main reason I come to church—especially since Dr. MacDougal started to shepherd this flock. That fight over last year's delegate to Council was enough to make a cynic out of the staunchest Christian. Some people say it's the reason that dear old Mr. Borden took to his heels and went up north to embrace James Bay and the Cree. But I have news for him. If he's searching for the Simple and Noble Savage, he won't find him, or even her. Human beings are human beings, be they rural or urban, white or brown, young or old, male or female— and not one of them is simple. Whether or not some of us are noble is still another question. And as for that politically incorrect word *savage,* try looking into the boardroom of any major corporation for some prime examples of the dictionary definition of savagery.

The twins are *both* kicking the pew ahead of them. A judgment on me for letting my mind wander from · celestial matters. There. A dig in Roland's ribs did the trick, who in turn dug Jerry. Whatever would a mother do without elbows? Boys are so much less complicated than girls. Good, bad; noisy, quiet; furious, joyful; black, white. None of this uneven ground in the middle, composed of gray—like fog. Girls are often so devious. Or maybe it's just being twins that makes the difference. Twins sail through their youth with built-in support systems. And what's Gillian got? Me, with whom she is currently on shaky ground. Donald, her father, with whom she disagrees on almost every issue. Her brothers, who tease her. A group of noisy giggling girls, who talk about boys and their own bodies and their teachers—in that order—almost exclusively. And her best friend, who stole her boyfriend last week.

Aha. So the theme this week is a double-barreled one: love and forgiveness. Not content with a gospel reading of the parable of the lost sheep, we are also being treated to the prodigal son. The lost sheep—the tale of a shepherd who leaves his ninety-nine sheep in the wilderness while he searches for the one who is lost. The prodigal son—that classic story of a parent's readiness to forgive a wayward child, and to overlook a worthy one in the process. I might just as well go home and check the roast. I have no problems with those two stories. For starters, I know what I'd do if any one of my three children was in grave danger. Suppose two of them were teetering on the edge of an erupting volcano when the other one fell into the lava. I'd dive right in after the child who had fallen. That's real basic animal mother stuff. A father would no doubt dive in, too, but he'd probably tuck the other two children in a safe cave before leaving. The real primal instinct for immediate action to protect her cubs comes from the mother bear.

And the prodigal son. Yes, sirree, if Gillian were to come home one day and say, "Mother, I'm really sorry I've been so bitchy and difficult lately. I wish I hadn't snapped at you so hard yesterday when you suggested I take my warm sweater to the football game. I love you in a different way now from when I was five years old, but I love you just as much"—why, I'd probably break her rib cage hugging her. I'd make her grasshopper pie for supper. I'd give her the biggest piece, and let Donald and the twins wait for seconds. And those three have been begging me for a grasshopper pie for six months.

That woman in the raccoon coat in the third row on the aisle seat. Never saw her before. All those delicate features and beautiful bones. A dead ringer for Mona. Startled, I bestow upon the stranger a surge of hostility—undeserved and intense.

Old Mona was never very easy to have for a sister. Pretty and slender, while I was built square and sensible—inside and out. Plus, she was older than me and knew all the ropes—which, in the freewheeling '60s, were complicated to untangle. Then Mona decided she wasn't satisfied with just the love beads and the ethnic dresses and the bare feet. Nor with the guitars and the folk songs, to which she knew all the words—and could sing them, too, in her high, thin, clear, and strangely lovely voice. No, she had to have it all. The motorcycles and the drugs and the shacking up. And Mom and Dad beside themselves with worry.

There were about five years there when they hardly knew I was around. But I was. Oh, how I was around. Home most of the time, hating Mona as she ran out to waiting cars and vans and Hondas, trailing her full skirts and her scarves and her flowers, snuggling up to scores of bewitched strangers whom we never met. And Mom fretting, evening after evening, peering through the drapes, walking the floor in her chenille dressing gown till four A.M., readjusting the ornaments on the mantel, chewing on her thumbnail, sometimes praying out loud. Then Mona'd be away days at a time, only to return with her beady little pupils staring. And there'd be love and concern all around for the plight she was in. When she left for good, with that traveling rock star, I saw my mother age ten years in one week.

But I can't pretend that I did any grieving when Mona took off. Peace, I thought, at last. With the competition gone, I gained some confidence, and boys began to shuffle around on the fringes of my life. By the time three years had passed, I was having a half-decent social life, and I was looking forward like crazy to my twenty-first birthday. My parents had agreed to rent the Oddfellows Hall for a real once-in-a-lifetime bash for me. A group was to come from Sellory Corners to play, and it looked as though half the town would show up to hear them.

It was the first time my parents had really let themselves go since Mona left, and it seemed as if they were prepared to make up for their neglect of me with one huge extravagant gesture. I was more than ready for that. I was weary of the daily ritual at the mailbox. "Nothing from Mona again? Oh dear God, where can she *be?*" Tears in the eyes, sagging shoulders, *every day*. And almost never did I hear, "And how are *you?*" So I was one hundred percent eager for that birthday party.

The night of the party, while I was having my bubble bath and fixing my hair, I was happy enough to blot out all those years of resentment. Mom had a new dress, and of course I did, too. My dad had bought each of us a corsage. No one mentioned Mona's absence. No one spoke about how lovely she had looked at twenty-one. It was as though, on that one exquisitely beautiful day of mine, she had never existed.

Ten minutes before we were to set out, the phone rang. There had been an accident on Highway 103, and Mona had been in one of the cars—obviously on her way home. Head injuries, they said, and a coma. She was in a hospital, a half hour's drive away.

My mom didn't even pause to put on her coat—although it was November—and flew out the door, corsage and all. Dad had already beat her to the car, and the engine was running—which I suppose nullifies everything I said about mother and father bears. It would have been good to hear, "So sorry, dear, but we have to go." But no. They just went. It was like the ninety-and-nine in the wilderness and the prodigal son rolled into one. The son had, after all, a brother who was a hotbed of jealousy, coveting the fatted calf, which, in his opinion, was being killed for the wrong person.

At first, I didn't know what to do. I may have been a late bloomer, but I was not stupid. I knew that if I went to my party and lived it up, if I had the kind of good time I had been dreaming about, everyone in town would be on Mona's side, with no votes cast for the callous sister. I could go to the party and radiate distress, but this would be only slightly more bearable than what I chose to do. Opting for the heroine's role, the part of the long-suffering sister—which I knew so well how to play—I took a taxi to the Oddfellows Hall and made an announcement over the P.A. system. There had been a terrible accident. There was no way I could desert my parents at a time like this. I therefore would be leaving in a few moments to join them at the hospital. But all the food was already prepared, and the group had begun tapping its collective feet. So live it up, friends. It won't do Mona any good to put on long faces. Thanks for coming to my party. Maybe the next time I turn twenty-one, I'll be able to join you. (Uneasy laughter.) So bye, folks. Thank you all for coming, and good night. Have fun.

I borrowed the Jamiesons' car and cried all the way to the hospital, and not for Mona, either. Of course it was rousing good fun in the emergency room. My mother sobbing and sobbing, picking petals out of the roses in her corsage. My father white and silent, staring straight ahead of him, holding Mom's hand. Me saying all the right things—the words I'd said so often. "Don't worry, Mom. She'll be OK. Mona has a way of landing on her feet."

But this time she had landed on her head, and it was twenty-five days before she regained consciousness. It wounds me still to remember the look of thundering joy on my mother's face when Mona finally opened her eyes and said, "Hi, folks," just like it was any old ordinary day. Both parents floated through that afternoon on a high that would have stood them in good stead at any of Mona's parties. Certainly I never saw either of them radiate that kind of walking ecstasy over anything that ever happened to *me*.

After that, of course, there followed a long, slow, and completely successful convalescence. Presents and flowers flowed in by the truckload. What's more, the weeks in the hospital broke Mona's drug habit enough for her to get a handle on it—and probably to take a good hard look at herself. When she was well, she stayed home long enough to make her peace with Mom and Dad, to give them a month of love and repentance to repay them for five long years of misery. And for them, that was enough. She didn't know she needed to make her peace with me. It never crossed her mind that I had suffered at her hands. It never crossed anyone's mind.

Then she went forth, our Mona, as Dr. MacDougal is advocating right now, to do all the perfect things. University. Marriage to a successful surgeon. Five beautiful children. Member of the Unitarian Church. Organizer of the United Appeal in her city. And still a beauty at forty-six.

So, Dr. MacDougal, what has this sermon of yours done for me? Forgiveness is a long, steep climb, and I'm not the first one in history to have resented the killing of a fatted calf. And I'm sure all those sheep found it pretty cold and lonely out there in the wilderness while the shepherd was looking for the one maverick that didn't have the sense or sensitivity to move with the flock. Don't ask me to neat up my past all in one sitting.

Besides, I think some of us really want to hug our hates close to ourselves, long after they cease to be valid. At least you've got to admit, Dr. MacDougal, that I'm thinking about it all again, which is something I haven't done for a long time.

And although this hour in church has served to open old wounds and to make my rage as fresh as dew, those few moments on the edge of the volcano did tell me a thing or two. My dad is dead, so it's too late for him. But I think I'll just go over and see Mom in East Jeddick this afternoon. It's not all that far, and I haven't seen her since last July. I feel a kind of longing for her. Maybe we can talk over old times a bit. I've never told her how I felt during those five long years. She probably doesn't even know why I sort of dropped out of her life. Perhaps I could say that being a mother is something we have in common. Maybe it's time I told her how much she hurt me. Because otherwise how is she going to understand why I suddenly so totally forgive her?

Twelve o'clock on the button. Here comes the Benediction and his weekly hope that the peace that passeth all understanding will come our way. But don't ask for everything all at once, Dr. MacDougal. Give me awhile to sort it all out. After all, it's only been twenty-two years. Just give me a little more time.

Elliot's Daughter

I HAVE DECIDED to keep a journal. Not a diary, exactly. An account of sorts—of my life and of my thoughts.

I am a writer—or so I like to call myself. Some writers refer to themselves as authors, but this is a pretentious term, and very few writers use it. Amateurs very frequently call themselves authors, but this is an almost sure sign of their inferior status. But I do not look upon myself as an amateur, in spite of the fact that my work has seldom been published—three times, if I must be absolutely honest: one short story in a South Shore contest (first prize), one article on the care and feeding of cats, and a poem entitled "Litany," which, to my great astonishment and delight, was accepted five years ago by a university literary magazine. It was this last triumph that I felt pushed me out of the amateur status and into the heady world of professionalism. After all, those literary journals are usually juried by English professors and established writers.

"Litany" was written in free verse—my first attempt at this form, or lack of it. Usually I am more at home with a regular meter and a predictable rhyme scheme. I am by nature an orderly and somewhat contained man (I almost said gentleman, but I realize that this word—in fact, this concept—is very much out of date), but I took considerable satisfaction from the fact that the words and the lines of my poem wandered (I was about to say jumped) all over the page, with a freedom that I would at one time have regarded as licentious. I'm sure I don't know what came over me that day. That night, actually. I do remember that I awakened in the middle of the night after a dream whose contents I could not or would not identify. All I recall is that I woke up in the grip of a terrible rage. Sleep was impossible—or maybe I was afraid to return to it—so I turned on the bed lamp and began to write. I let my fury carry me along (there was no possibility of recollecting anything in tranquility that night) and the result was truly extraordinary. When I re-read it in the morning, I could scarcely believe that it was I who had written it. It wasn't just the form that was out of character—all those staggering lines and dancing words. The content was bizarre also. It was full of profanity and a great deal of unbridled sex. I could only dimly remember having written it. It was like the memory of some fevered fiction that occurs during a grave illness.

But even in the cold dawn of the next day, I was able to see that the poem was good. I could not honestly recognize what it meant, what the poet (I) was communicating. But I sensed a kind of profundity lurking somewhere within or between the lines. Consciously hurrying lest I change my mind, I scrabbled around in my desk until I found a suitable envelope. Then I typed out the poem—with all its strange pauses and detours intact—wrote a brief covering letter, and addressed it to the editor of a quite prestigious academic journal, complete with SASE. You see? In spite of my less than spectacular publishing record, I know the proper procedure, as well as the correct terminology that goes along with it. Self-Addressed Stamped Envelope. For rejections, about which I know a great deal.

And that is not all about which I am knowledgeable. Always a clean copy. Generous margins. Page numbers in the top right-hand corner. No staples. And so on.

May 6

Let me tell you a bit about myself. I have said *you,* because when one writes in a diary or a journal one certainly has a sense of speaking to someone. Not to one-self, and not to any real person. But undeniably a person, perhaps a mythical one. But to continue: I am unmarried, forty-three years of age, a postal clerk. Because I work in a small substation of the postal system, I have become familiar with some of the people who live in that area of the city. One of these people is a writer. His name is Elliot Archer. I'm sure you will have heard of him. He writes novels, the occasional excellent short story, some-times a poem. I follow his career with great interest, for obvious reasons. Profiles of his life and work appear in local and national newspapers. Even Peter Gzowski has seen fit to interview him. He actually supports himself on his writing. He has no other job. This is practically unheard of in the writing world, and impresses me deeply. Almost all of us must have other forms of em-ployment if we are to avoid starvation. Not he. He lives simply—I have searched out his home and inspected it, assessing its worth, envying him his independence and his success. His house is small and would benefit from a coat of paint. It is in an undistinguished part of the city. But he owns it (I've checked on that, also), and it is free of any debilitating mortgage.

Elliot Archer is also not dying of hunger, for I have seen him myself in the local supermarket, his cart as full of food as anyone else's. I always take note of what he buys, and certain items keep reappearing with an intriguing regularity. He has a chronic fondness for Sara Lee chocolate cakes, ripple potato chips, black olives, Oreo cookies, and tonic water. It is a rare day, indeed, when one sees a head of lettuce or a good red tomato in his cart. He is fat and puffy looking, and his color is not good. I also have to say that he often appears ill-tempered—or possibly just plagued by anxiety.

Anxiety. I find myself asking, as I follow him from frozen foods to baked goods to dairy products (of which he buys very little), why or how can such a man be anxious? I watch those Express Mail items come sailing in for him week after week, with the names of this publisher and that celebrity written on their backs. Proofs? Essential correspondence? Notices of grants or awards or foreign sales? I would be frozen with shock were I to receive a parcel or letter by way of Express Mail. But he picks them up, heavy-lidded with boredom (or tiredness, maybe—I must be fair), looks casually at the back to verify the sender, mutters his thanks, and bumbles off toward the entrance. To home, then, to read his important mail over a gin and tonic or a Sara Lee cake. While I remain behind my counter, stripping off stamps, writing money orders, taking out my frustrations with the thump of the date stamp. It makes me angry that he does not seem more pleased to be Elliot Archer.

May 10

Let me speak a bit more about Elliot. (I've come to call him by his first name in the privacy of my own mind.) I don't know whether or not he is married. The interviews mention his career but not his domestic arrangements. But he is always alone when I see him. Either his wife is an invalid, stuffed away like Rochester's crazed spouse in some back room of his little house, or she is dead, or else perhaps he has chosen to remain single. Like me.

But that is not entirely accurate. I have not exactly chosen to remain a bachelor. I am full of fantasies that endow me with literary successes and a plethora of Express Mail envelopes. But certainly another of my dreams includes a cozy house (with multi-paned windows, shutters, a small neat garden) and a warm and loving wife (a pretty, smiling face in the doorway, the smell of muffins reaching me before I even open the gate, someone to whom I can read my first drafts). But obtaining that pretty and smiling wife has not proved to be an easy matter.

I am not handsome, nor have I ever been what one would call attractive. Or so I was led to believe by my father. And by my brother, Victor, whose physical and intellectual perfections were my own personal trial by fire during the sixteen long years when we inhabited the same house. I will admit, in the privacy of this journal, that it is not easy to be related to someone who does almost nothing wrong—except, of course, taunting and belittling his little brother, which were his two favorite and secret flaws. But quite apart from that, how can you compete with someone who comes first in every exam, who is captain of the school hockey team, who is equipped with broad shoulders (as early as the age of ten), smoldering eyes, and a shock of unruly black hair. I am of medium height, medium coloring, medium intelligence, medium athletic ability. If I robbed a bank at the height of noon without a mask and ran off with a bagful of money, the police would never find me. I look like too many other people—bland, featureless, even lacking the distinction of compelling ugliness, like Elliot Archer's. He looks a bit like a distinguished rhinoceros—bumbling and gross, but with a face and form that one would never, under any circumstances, forget.

It has been my misfortune in life to envy a lot of people—my brother, all members of the school hockey team, movie stars, those who excel at Trivial Pursuit, all published writers. When my father first told me that I was just about as distinguished as a jellyfish (and then punched me jovially and laughed, apparently surprised that I was not more amused), I believed what he said. "Gotta be able to take a joke, son," he'd say every time he introduced the jellyfish theme—which was often. A jellyfish—if you've never seen one—is flat and colorless, moves in an indeterminate way that suggests a deficiency of purpose or direction, and lacks a spine. On the frequent occasions when I was likened to a jellyfish, I would grind my teeth (which I visualized as being worn down to flat nubbins, all twenty-eight of them) and tell myself that a common jellyfish is closely related to a Portuguese man-of-war; it simply lacks the color and the long poisonous stingers. But even as I thought this, I knew that the differences were more significant than the similarities. A jellyfish just sort of galumphs through the water. A man-of-war, with its long, rhythmically swaying streamers, is a floating menace, possessed of a strange and dangerous beauty.

My mother? A gentle and ineffectual woman, who deplored the way I was put down by my father, but who did nothing to prevent it. But, to be fair to that long-suffering lady, I will say that on the rare occasions when she limped to my defense, the fallout was more painful and probably more damaging to me than its original source. Father's rage was fierce at such times. She was turning the boy against him. She was a wimp, herself, and to hell with her opinion. How could she expect the boy to develop backbone if she rushed to protect him from the perfectly normal give-and-take of daily life? It crossed my mind that it was he that was doing the giving, while I was in perpetual charge of the taking. But of course I said nothing. He had high blood pressure, and we were supposed to keep this in mind.

These journal conversations are long ones. It occurs to me that I may be writing a diary in order to avoid writing anything else.

May 11

I see that yesterday's entry was intended to be a commentary on my marital state. But I was sidetracked by domestic confessions. A discussion of family frailties is a hard subject to leave.

I cannot remember a time when I liked Victor. I suppose this means that he started his attacks upon me very early. No doubt he pinched me as I lay in my baby carriage. He would have enjoyed that. But the memory of things he did—small things, maybe even unintentional things—still has the power to hurt me at the age of forty-three. I recall making a lawn ornament. I had laboriously cut out the form from a discarded piece of wood, and painted the result. I thought it was a thing of wonder, and asked my mother if I might stick it in the lawn. Yes, I could. She told me it was lovely. I was beside myself with pride and deep contentment. After my brother saw it, he retired to the basement, remaining down there for five hours. It was a Saturday, and it was raining. On Sunday, the smell of fresh paint wafted up to the main floor. Innocent fool that I was, I had no idea what he was doing. On Monday morning, there they were, apparently put out the night before—three more lawn ornaments, perfectly cut, perfectly painted, perfectly placed.

I left the house that morning with my father and Victor. "Aha!" exclaimed my father, his face alive with smiles. "That's the way to do it!" Then he stopped in front of my ornament, threw back his head, and roared with laughter. When he finished with his awful mirth, he turned to me and said, "Well, it's important to try." He patted me vaguely on the head. To Victor he said, "Good work, my son!"

That afternoon, when no one was at home, I went out to the front lawn and savagely pulled my ornament out of the ground. Wrapping it in a brown paper bag, I walked the half mile down to the harbor and threw it into the sea.

Eventually, Victor dealt me the bitterest blow that he could possibly have devised. He died. At the age of eighteen, in the prime of his young manhood—tall, athletic, pursued by more young women than he could possibly accommodate, headed for law school, adored by his parents—he contracted meningitis and was dead within a week.

My parents' grief was so absolute that I felt annihilated by it. In that one week, they lost both of their sons, although they were not aware of this at the time. My brother's perfection was now embalmed. From now on, my father would compare me with Victor with even less mercy. Placed beside his dreams of what my brother might have become was the reality of what I was. I would remain forever the jellyfish to Victor's man-of-war. I would never, ever, as long as I lived, be able to surpass my brother in anything at all. His death deprived me of this, and I hated him for it.

Picture me, then, at the age of sixteen, destined to be second-rate for the rest of my life. But ultimately a wife would have helped. Or even, when still young, just an adoring girlfriend. But adoring girls did not surround me like swarming flies, as they had done to Victor. I was attracted to the wrong girls—to the school stars, the cheerleaders, the bright and flashy ones. My advances to them were shy and uncertain, and no one flew into my arms. Looking back now, I think they probably didn't even know I was advancing. "Not much of a stud," said my father. "Not like Victor."

May 29

I have learned that Elliot Archer is—or was—a married man. Today he came to the postal station to buy a Priority Mail envelope. "For Geraldine," he said, turning to a friend in the line. "I have to let her know if I have room for her. She'd like to come in on the Monday train. Just a short visit. To lick her wounds."

Geraldine? I tried to keep my mind on the ripping of stamps and the making of change, without impeding my efforts to hear everything. *Licking her wounds?*

"What a helluva month for a daughter to choose to come visiting!"

A daughter! The man was unjustly blessed—not only with a successful writing career, but with a daughter as well.

"That will be $6.41," I said to my customer, as Elliot talked on.

"If she can't keep her marriage intact, she needn't think she can come crawling back into the nest. He wasn't *my* choice. And she says she'll be here for twelve days. Wants to be out of town while some legal wrangling is taking place. Goddamn time to pick! Revisions due on one book in three weeks, and the proofs of my other one arriving in the next couple of days. Couldn't be a worse time for me to have to act like a father." He muttered something under his breath and heaved an enormous sigh. "She can come, but I absolutely refuse to have my concentration interfered with." He stepped up to the counter as my other customer moved away.

"One Priority Mail envelope," he said. "And twenty regular stamps."

I swallowed. "You'd be more sure of it arriving quickly if you sent it by Express Mail," I offered.

He looked at me sharply. "Too bloody expensive," he growled. He turned to his friend. "Priority Mail will probably get it to Toronto on time, and if it doesn't, it's not my problem. Hasn't she ever heard of the telephone?"

And haven't *you?* I countered, but not, of course, aloud.

Tonight I have but one wish. That it be necessary for Geraldine to put something into the mail when she comes for a visit. I want to see what Elliot has produced in the way of a child. Something cranky and swarthy, I expect. Egotistical and assertive. But on the other hand, anyone who rushes for refuge to a man like Elliot must be in a pretty desolate condition.

June 4

My complaints to you have been mainly about my father and my brother. But it was really my mother who kept me from marrying. She unmercifully criticized the only two girls I brought home for her approval. "Not good enough for you," she declared, clinging to her one remaining child, in spite of his inadequacies. Also, I think she was taking this opportunity to assert herself in a significant way, in an area where she could actually exercise some control. I can forgive her for this, because I'm able to see that she must have been starved almost to death with a hunger to control something or somebody. Maybe I didn't recognize—at that time—all the facets of her disapproval of those two girls. Sometimes I don't even really know what is going on in my own head until I write it all down. Anyway, for whatever reason—habit, maybe—fear, perhaps—I listened to her, both times. And I acquiesced.

Not until I was thirty-five years old did I leave home.

No doubt you find that difficult to believe. Every time I would announce my intention to leave, my mother would burst into tears and sob, "Don't leave me! Don't leave me!" I knew perfectly well what she meant by that. She meant: "Don't leave me alone with your father." What does a jellyfish do when a current is running so strongly in one direction? But two weeks after my mother died, I moved from Victoria to Halifax, putting an entire continent between my father and me.

June 7

I saw Geraldine today. She was in the grocery store with her father. She has a small, tidy face, large brown eyes, and absolutely straight light brown hair. Beside Elliot, she looked beige all over. Although he was dressed in black, the color that came to mind was red. He looked that intense. Thinking about his proofs, I thought, my heart squeezed with envy. Proofs should be a cause for great joy. Proofs mean that a book is on its way. Unbeetle your brow, I demanded. Your daughter is with you. Your book is coming.

Geraldine looked full of anxiety. If you were desperate enough to flee to Elliot Archer for comfort, I thought, what on earth kind of trauma did you leave behind? Maybe tomorrow you will need some stamps.

June 9

Today she came and bought a small package of stamped envelopes. I smiled at her as I handed her the change. Timidly, sadly, she smiled back. A warm light softened and brightened her tight little face. I felt something inside me lurch convulsively. This girl was not the kind who usually attracted me. No color. No flash. She was very small. Why was I finding it necessary to lean against the counter and to breathe deeply?

Her name is Geraldine, I mused. Elliot would have preferred a son and would have named him Gerald. Why could he not have named her Sylvia or Anne or Madeline? Why did he have to enshrine his preference in her name, for all to see?

"Thank you," she said, and left. Her voice was husky and very gentle.

June 11

Last night I couldn't sleep, so eventually I decided to make use of my insomnia instead of fighting it. At 3:15 A.M., I shuffled over to my desk, pulled my paper and pen from the drawer, and started to write. I was very, very tired by the time I began, and my usual constraints were abandoned. I felt exhausted, dispirited, reckless. In that state of mind, I wrote a love poem—for whom and to whom, I did not bother to inquire. I just wrote it.

After a brief sleep, I rose at seven A.M., showered, shaved, and reread the poem. It was very good. The subject of the poem was quite clearly Geraldine.

Today she didn't come into the post office. Elliot said she would be home for twelve days. Hastily I counted off the days on my fingers. Six down and six to go. Not much time. I feel something akin to panic.

June 13

I'm not sleeping much at all this week. The long nights are spent in an angry replay of my past and in a dispirited contemplation of my future. I have read that a mentally healthy person has an eager and positive attitude toward the present. But, try as I will, I cannot see that the present has much to offer me. I try all the gimmicks and ploys suggested by Sunday school and the *Reader's Digest*. I address myself sternly: Think positively. You are not hungry. You do not live in a war-torn zone. You are not a paraplegic. You dwell in a beautiful city of tree-lined streets and charming old houses, surrounded on three sides by views of the sea. Although your father left bruises on your spirit, he left none on your body. It is almost summertime, and the air is very soft. You are a writer, and you have just written an excellent poem. You have reason to rejoice.

But rejoice I cannot. This is Day 8, and Geraldine

has not reappeared. I have done what I can to make this happen. I have searched the mailbags for Express Mail envelopes and Priority Mail items, which I would be quite prepared to deliver by hand, in spite of the irregularities of such a move. I've traveled up and down Elliot's street several times, exercising Mrs. Harvey's golden retriever in order to give a certain legitimacy to this unaccustomed walking to and fro. I've spent an inordinate amount of time in the supermarket, knowing that although a person can live ten days without stamps, the need for food is a different matter altogether. But Geraldine probably does the grocery shopping while I'm at work. Once this week I saw Elliot. He was lumbering through the streets, hands clasped behind his back, head down. And mumbling. No doubt he was composing.

If I see her, I will do something. I don't yet know what I will do. But it will be something. I think of those girls in high school who didn't even know I was pursuing them when I made my shy advances. I am determined that this will not happen again. I am forty-three. I will not ever be young again, and I am marching slowly but unavoidably in the direction of fifty. I am feeling a fear of something that is even more compelling than my shyness. Yes, if given the opportunity, I will certainly do something.

In the meantime, in the brief intervals between stamps and registrations and money orders, I think about Geraldine's startlingly clean, shoulder-length, light brown, straight, beautiful hair. I want to touch it, and I know that it will be warm and slippery in its fineness. She looks to be about thirty-five. Not too late to bear a child. I am pleased that we look enough alike to be sister and brother. The child will resemble both of us. I can feel myself smiling tenderly as I put yet another parcel on the scales. "Will this be regular or expedited mail?" I say to the man who handed it to me, regarding this stranger with real affection. I can see that a heavy rain is falling. I think about how beautiful it looks, and I admire the wet faces of my customers as they approach the counter.

June 14

I saw her again today. I saw Geraldine. She was wandering about the drugstore in which my postal station is located. In spite of all my resolutions to act decisively should she reappear, I was powerless to do a single thing. I was trapped behind my counter—a half hour before my scheduled coffee break—with a long line of customers facing me. But their needs were uncomplicated—no registered letters, no parcels for Hong Kong—and I was free to watch her. She moved up and down the aisles, gazing at displays of Band-Aids, cold remedies, baby powder, vitamins, greeting cards. But she touched nothing, bought nothing. Killing time, I thought, as I weighed a small package. Then she stopped before a display of bubble bath concoctions, picking one bottle off the shelf, inspecting the label, checking the price, putting it back. Too expensive? Too self-indulgent a substance to pour into a bathtub owned by Elliot Archer? She touched the bottle again—almost tenderly, I felt—before walking away. I visualized her immersed in a thick cloud of bubbles, just one small knee partly visible, her eyes closed.

She must have sensed that I was watching her. Slowly, she looked up and met my eyes. Then she smiled and raised her right hand in a tentative half-wave. Clutching a five-dollar bill, I held up my own hand.

My customer coughed, and I handed him his change.

I want to order a whole case of that bubble bath and leave it on Elliot's veranda.

June 15

Not a good day. No sign, no sight of Geraldine.

June 16

Where can she be? I patrol the neighborhood during my lunch hour and after five. I buy groceries twice daily. I walk Mrs. Harvey's dog. All to no avail. Maybe she left sooner than she planned.

June 17

I saw her from afar today. She was sitting on a bench in the Public Gardens, hands clasped in her lap, looking straight ahead, her huge eyes like stones. I had brought my sandwich over at noontime, to eat beside the duck pond. It was Day 12, and I had hoped that I might be cheered up by the swans, the flowers, the muddy little lake, even the pigeons.

When I saw her, I reacted exactly as I would have done at sixteen or seventeen. My legs felt as though they no longer belonged to me, and my breathing was painful and short. I held on to the back of a park bench in order to steady myself and to plan my strategy. For she was alone. A merciful Providence had delivered unto me this miracle.

But no. It appeared that Providence had done no such thing. Coming along the path from the canteen was Elliot, stomping along between the flower beds, armed with two ice cream cones, one large, one small. I sat down on the bench and watched them, systematically feeding my entire lunch to the muttering pigeons.

Elliot handed her the small ice cream and began to pace up and down in front of the bench, gesticulating angrily. I couldn't hear what he was saying, but the tone was unmistakable. He pointed at her, at the sky, at himself, and clenched his fat fist. He took frequent bites of his large ice cream, cramming it into his mouth and then talking with his mouth full. Geraldine sat in exactly the same position as before, except that she held the ice cream in both hands, not eating it. Gradually it started to melt, and although it began to run down between her fingers, she paid no attention to it.

My mind was full of urgent fantasies. I felt that her chest must be close to suffocation, pressured by a high-pitched unexpressed howl. She must want to kill him, I insisted, to claw at his eyes, to draw blood. In that moment, I felt I understood everything there was to know about hate, and possibly about murder.

Another concept presented itself to me, and I was stunned by the force of its clarity. She loves him. She probably hates him, but she loves him, too. I thought about my own father, and realized that most of my pain derived not from the rage I had felt but from the unreturned love that was rotting away in my heart. I could hardly bear to look at the corollary to that discovery— that possibly many or most of the children who suffer at the hands of their parents love them, somewhere deep down beneath the brittle surface of their hatred. The whipped, the abandoned, the sexually abused, the insulted, the neglected, the ridiculed—they all want, most of all, for their parents to appear in the doorway and say, "I love you. I honor you. You are of value to me." And best of all: "I'm sorry." And if that happened, what an avalanche of forgiveness would be let loose upon the world.

The outrageous injustice of such a quick and easy forgiveness stabbed me. A fresh and unfamiliar kind of anger possessed me.

Even as I reacted to those thoughts, Geraldine rose from the bench, neck stiff, hands dripping, and walked slowly toward the large wrought-iron garden gates. Her ice cream lay on the path, attacked by pigeons; her father, at last speechless, was staring after her, his face angry and desolate.

I wrote a poem when I returned home this evening. I called it "Love and Hate," but it lacked what literary critics used to call decorum. I think I know what I want to say, but it will take awhile—some recollection perhaps, some tranquility—before I can convert that raw emotion into something that contains more art than therapy.

June 19

Elliot seems to be writing letters again, because today he has twice visited the post office. My own writing is not going well. I am very depressed.

July 4

It is now Day 17. I count each day now in terms of how much time has gone by since Geraldine left. I may stop writing this journal. I seem to have learned from it nothing at all.

July 5

Nothing at all.

July 6

This has been a difficult day for me. I thought I saw Geraldine. I was *sure* I saw her. I was cashing a check at the Bank of Nova Scotia on Spring Garden Road when I looked out the window and saw a small person disappear around the corner. Same size, same sleek brown hair, same carriage, the same way of moving. Or so—for one electric instant—I thought. Then sanity returned, and I reminded myself that she has been back in Toronto for nineteen long days. I could feel myself blushing as I accepted my money from the cashier.

July 7

I miss the satisfaction and the release of writing about my memories and my thoughts. But at the moment I seem to have only one thought worth expressing. And giving voice to it gives me no release, no satisfaction.

July 13

Today Elliot approached my counter in the company of one of his friends. I have often felt that this man should have no friends whatsoever. He is undeserving of such blessings. But we must not waste our energies groping for evidences of justice in this life. Besides, Elliot has many faces, many masks. I have observed this. He smiles affably at his friends. He dredges up humor from heaven knows what secret places in his mind. His jokes are funny. I have sometimes felt in danger of laughing.

Listen to this: I heard him say, "I don't know why she didn't return to Toronto. When she's that far away, I seldom think about her. Goddamnit, anyway." Then he paid for his stamps, stuffed them in his pocket, and was gone.

July 25

By means of judicious eavesdropping, I have discovered that although Geraldine has left her father's home, she has not vanished altogether off the face of the earth. She has moved to a room in another part of the city. If I wait long enough, and if I listen very attentively, I will discover where she is. Maybe Elliot will hand in a letter directed to her new address—a check, perhaps, or a note of apology. Even if it contains accusations and anger, I will have learned her last name and where to find her. And then I will know exactly what to do.

I see Elliot often. He still eats Sara Lee chocolate cake and dilutes his gin with tonic. His brows continue to be drawn together in either anxiety or displeasure, and there is no spring in his step as he shuffles along. Express Mail parcels continue to arrive, as do registered letters. These he receives without the faintest sign of delight or even of curiosity. He seems not yet to have written a letter to his daughter. This is discouraging, but not overwhelmingly so. The present is now full of challenges and possibilities. I greet the start of each day with enormous interest.

Mrs. MacIntosh

Even when Thomas is standing up, his stomach strains against his vest, so you can imagine what it is like when he is sitting down. Normally I have nothing whatsoever against obesity. In fact, there is a comfortable and soft quality about large bodies that I often find appealing. But it is never easy to tolerate pomposity, and I have always felt that a pompous person who is fat is the least attractive kind. If a man is constantly nagging you about your lack of self-discipline, it is irritating to realize that he has no discipline at all in the matter of food. And Thomas has an irritating habit of scratching that stomach in a slow and thoughtful way just before delivering one of his ponderous pronouncements.

As when he said to me one evening at dinner, over the chicken casserole, "Alfreda, I have decided, after careful consideration, that it is time I purchased a new

suit, possibly two. The caliber of my professionalism re-
quires that my clothing complement my position at the
bank. I feel that the quality of a suit reflects the level of
one's expertise." All this preceded by that vague, un-
functional scratching.

In the old days when I was younger, when my eyes
were shut tight and all critical faculties dormant, I would
have thought, Yes, indeed, an important job needs an
important suit. At what point in a marriage, I wonder,
does one start to watch and see and to feel a drawing
away? I suppose it varies. In some cases, no doubt, it
never happens at all. But how can you live with someone
seven days a week for eleven years without eventually
spotting, for instance, that he has no idea who he really
is? "Take off your mask!" I have sometimes longed to
scream. "Take a good look and then do some heavy
stocktaking."

But Thomas's stocktaking was of a different kind, and
my screams have always been imaginary.

His mother, I am told, would never permit anyone
to call him Tommy or Tom. Mrs. MacIntosh was quick
to point out that her father's name had been Thomas
MacGregor, and she made it very clear that her respect
for his memory was profound. You did not dillydally
with Mrs. MacIntosh, even in the matter of names. The

first time Thomas took me home to meet her, he introduced me with pride. I was seventeen to his twenty-six, and I was pretty; neither of these facts did anything to increase my popularity with her.

"Mother," he said, puffing himself up even then like a pigeon—although this only occurred to me much later—"I take pleasure in introducing Freddie. Freddie, I'd like you to meet my mother."

She rose from her needlepoint chair, erect and uncompromising, looking at me carefully from tip of scruffed shoes to kinky perm. She smiled a narrow company smile and said, "I'm delighted to meet you. Freddie? Did you say Freddie?"

"Alfreda is her real name," Thomas said. "Her friends call her Freddie."

"Alfreda is a lovely name," she said, coolly. "I will call you Alfreda."

Oh well, I thought, it probably doesn't matter in the slightest, because I can see that you are not likely to be numbered among my friends.

Which turned out to be true. I never did get rid of the sense that my social slip was showing, that I was exactly what she never, in her most reckless moment, would have chosen for a daughter-in-law. To her, I was a piece of insubstantial fluff, blown in from the Yukon, where my father worked as a laborer on a weather station. And I *was* insubstantial. I was torn in too many directions. I raged against my father's drinking bouts, and wished he would clean his fingernails and rein in his temper. I also faulted my mother for not making some of these things happen. But I respected my father's hard work and his fierce pride, and I loved my mother. I swayed with whatever wind blew hardest.

"And just who does that woman think she is, anyway?" I would whisper aloud when I was back in my rooming house, soaking in the tub. A MacGregor by birth and a MacIntosh by marriage, but from an inferior part of town—no better than my own—and a widow at that. No man to back up all those pretensions with a wallet or a profession. A front porch that needs painting. I would immerse myself in the hot water and blow a volley of bubbles.

I suppose I was so taken up with Mrs. MacIntosh's glacial pride that I failed to notice that her son shared some of her less attractive characteristics. It was not easy to connect these two people, at first. They looked as though they had not one single gene in common. She was tall and pencil thin. He was of middling height and stocky, muscular and sturdy. The stomach came much later, after he placed three thousand miles between his mother and himself. She would never for one second have permitted that paunch to develop.

But it was his face that was a lie to his parentage. It was round and pleasant; as a small child, he must have been unusually attractive—a dead ringer for any Campbell Soup Kid. There was no way for me to know that with the passage of years he would look more and more like a Pekingese dog. Nor, under different circumstances, would I have minded that fact. But, when you marry a man with a pleasant round face who is kind and attentive, it is a shock to discover, after a while, that you are being treated very sternly by someone who resembles a Pekingese dog.

Pride sits badly on any face, but some people have the looks that can carry arrogance and conceit with a kind of flair. Like Mrs. MacIntosh. Much as I feared and disliked my future mother-in-law, it was not difficult to recognize that she had class. She didn't need wealth in order to make her point in our community. And the point that she obviously wanted to make was that she had come from superior stock. Her posture was not merely flawless. It proclaimed to all who saw her that she was proud of who and what she was. You had to check a tendency to curtsy when she entered a room. What's more, she had the looks to go with this. When I first saw her, I suppose she was about forty-two, and a very young forty-two at that. Her eyes were gray and clear, her nose slender in the bridge, delicately aquiline, straight out of a Van Dyck painting. Her cheekbones were well defined, her chin firm. Her neck was long and still lovely. Crowning all this was a head of prematurely white hair, thick, wavy, elegantly arranged. It mattered not at all that she had only two formal outfits. Had she worn either of them to a Buckingham Palace garden party, heads would have turned. As I looked at her, even at the time of that unfortunate meeting, I kept repeating to myself, *good blood, good blood*. And although I feared and abhorred what Mrs. MacIntosh represented, I longed to possess that same sure and heady confidence: I wanted to have a share in her legacy.

Of course Mrs. MacIntosh resisted the match with every weapon at her disposal. And her weapons were deadly. Her insults were delivered with a smile—subtle affronts disguised as compliments. If you would like to know how this is done, stand in front of a mirror and smile graciously. Then, maintaining the smile, strive to look superior, pained, and disapproving, all at the same time. She had mastered this technique to perfection. And if I turned up for dinner in my very best dress, purchased especially for the occasion, she could be guaranteed to

say something like, "Your shoes are unusually shiny tonight, Alfreda" (smile, smile). This could be interpreted
in various ways:

—Shiny shoes are invariably made of plastic or of
leather of an inferior quality, or

—Your shoes are usually not shined properly, or

—I am commenting on your shoes in order to avoid
mentioning your unfortunate dress.

Or she would say, casually, to Thomas, "Whatever
happened to that strikingly beautiful Rose Harrigan? The
one who won the scholarship to Oxford? Alfreda, now,
has much better skin than Rose." Which could be de-
coded as "Alfreda is not strikingly beautiful, nor has she
won any scholarships lately."

Nonetheless, before I reached my nineteenth birthday, Thomas and I did marry. He was in the grip of a
wild infatuation. I suppose I attracted him because I was
so unlike that domineering force who was his mother. I
was soft-spoken and self-effacing, a person who had not
yet grown into her skin. I was not at all sure who I was,
and this must have appealed strongly to the MacIntosh
desire to mold, to instruct, to control. As I look at old
photographs, I can also see that I was attractive and smiling and had a good figure. This apparently added up to
something he was willing to fight for. At any rate, at the

very moment of highest tension in the MacIntosh household, his bank transferred him to a small community in New Brunswick, 3,200 miles from his home in Alberta. We went downtown together that afternoon. He bought the license, and I bought a white dress. The night before we boarded the train for our long journey east, we were married in the MacIntosh living room beside the needle-point chair. His mother held a small stiff reception, and was gracious and smiling throughout, her eyes icy cold.

In the beginning, in our short freedom from responsibility, Thomas had known how to laugh and have fun. As long as he was fighting to possess me, he made me feel desirable, sought after, worthy. But almost from the moment he realized I was securely and irrevocably his, he started to examine me for flaws. Brainwashing always tells, and his mother's standards of behavior and dress and speech were etched more deeply upon him than anything I could possibly provide. Besides, he was ambitious, and it was essential that I should not hinder his progress. He watched me carefully, and did not always like what he saw. This scrutiny hurt me long before it started to anger me, and by then the habit of silence was strong.

At first I felt that his criticisms were justified, and his newly acquired dignity impressed and intrigued me. I was young, and I was neither MacGregor nor MacIntosh. He was twenty-eight and an upwardly mobile bank employee. I could appreciate his desire to have me conform to his standards, which I assumed to be superior to mine. I felt branded by the Yukon and my father's blue collar. "If you please, Alfreda," Thomas would say, very cool, no fireworks. "Not that dress tonight. The Ryans know the most influential people in Woodstock. Wear your black. With the pearls I gave you for your birthday." I was still in love. If he had asked me to attend the party in a tiara, I might not have argued.

However, criticism, unless propped up by praise, impairs more often than it improves. According to him, I may have lacked class, a good background, advanced schooling, and discretion (one of his favorite words). I did not, however, lack intelligence. And ironically, the more he reproved and corrected me, the more I came to value my own upbringing and my own roots. After a time, I emerged from my blinkered condition. Suddenly one day, without warning, I looked around and said, out loud, "Who is this man I live with?" Once you have taken that first step, it is almost impossible to turn back.

I remember our first meal after asking that crucial question. I looked down at the end of the dining-room table and there, flanked by my two sons, was a Pekingese dog. And he was speaking.

"I know you will feel some pride, Alfreda," he said, coughing delicately into his fist, "when I tell you that the bank has seen fit to recognize my long years of service—useful and devoted ones, I might add."

I clasped my hands under the table. Why in heaven's name, I thought, does he always address me as though he were giving a speech to the Chamber of Commerce?

"That's nice, dear," I said.

"I am being transferred to Fredericton," he said, patting his mouth delicately with his napkin. "A very great honor. You will have the distinction, at long last, of being the wife of a manager of one of our nation's oldest banks. We move by the end of the month." He looked around the table, as though inviting applause.

Harold, age five, was already crying into his lamb chop. "Jimmy doesn't live in Fredericton," he sobbed. "I don't wanna live there. Please, Daddy. Tell them you won't go."

Young Thomas, mercifully nicknamed Tosh, was seven years old, and knew that a MacIntosh never cries. But his eyes were wide and bright, and his teeth were digging into his lower lip.

"Now, now, now, boys," purred Thomas Senior, scratching his vest, "congratulate your father. Fredericton is a much more impressive place in which to live than this small town. Why, it is the capital city of our province. And your father will be a very important man. This is cause for rejoicing, not for tears. Alfreda, point out to your children the wisdom and honor of this move. And you, my dear, will certainly have to pull up your socks now that we are heading for high places."

I, who had been pulling up my socks for nine years, saw no cause to rejoice. A familiar knot was forming somewhere just south of my rib cage.

"Congratulations, Thomas," I said.

We moved into the bank manager's house on a foggy May day. The house was small, and the branch tiny. Nonetheless, one could tell by Thomas's posture, by the set of his chins, that he felt the top of the mountain was in sight.

"Why do you want this so much?" I asked him that evening after the boys were in bed. "Why do you want so badly to be important, Thomas?" I had never before asked such a question, and I saw my hand shaking as I turned on the lamp by his chair.

"I consider that to be an impertinent and irrelevant question," he said, and rose stiffly to leave the room. Later, however, when the electric blanket was turned on and the lights were out, he said, "Mother always made it clear to me that I must aim for the top. She bought me educational toys. She scolded me if my marks were low. She pointed out that a MacIntosh must never take second place to anyone. She said that my father would agree, if he were living. She bought me books every Christmas, stories about great men. She said that this is what he would have chosen for me." He mumbled something.

"Pardon?" I asked.

I could barely hear him. "Every year I used to hope I'd get a teddy bear."

My heart lurched. Optimist that I was, I thought I was on the brink of meeting the real person who was my husband.

He continued. "And Alfreda," he said, once more addressing the Chamber of Commerce, "you will of course understand that you'll have to choose your friends with extreme care. A bank manager cannot be too cautious. You must realize that it is a position of enormous trust. We can't be entertaining just any old riffraff in this house."

I turned over to face the wall.

Five years passed, the boys grew older, and Thomas and I continued to live together and apart in the same house.

Although he was watchful of me and critical of my short-comings, I'm sure that he looked upon himself as an excellent father and husband. In his own cool way, he probably loved us—if you can love people without making the slightest effort to know them. Once I said to him, "Thomas, I wish you'd have a talk with Tosh. He's twelve now and seems awfully worried about something."

"Worried!" he exclaimed, clearing his throat, caressing his buttons. "Let him try for just one day to cope with *my* worries and he'd see how insignificant his own small troubles are. I'd like to watch him coping with fluctuating interest rates. You're the mother. Children are your territory. You speak to him. But no mollycoddling, mind! A MacIntosh must stand up to life without flinching."

A MacIntosh, indeed. After he left for work, I plunged my fist into a cushion, then threw it at the wall. I looked at the picture of his mother that stood on the mantel, and thought: Not one visit from that woman in fourteen years, and yet she is as present in this room as if she were sitting in that chair. I picked up another cushion and threw it at the chair. Then I went upstairs and cried for ten minutes. My tears were for all of us—for Tosh and his anxieties, for Harold and what was expected of him, for me and my new frustrations, for Thomas and the stranglehold his mother still had on him. Somewhere, I thought, somewhere inside of him there must be a real person, but whoever he is, he's locked in there too tightly ever to get out. I went downstairs to pick up the cushions and to vacuum the living-room carpet. We were having bank company for dinner that evening.

In May of that year I fell off a stool when I was spring-cleaning and broke my leg. For two whole months I was unable to keep the house as clean as a bank manager's house must be. So I engaged a cleaning lady to help me—a stout little woman called Geneva. She was originally from Saint John and was married to a sergeant at the nearby Gagetown base. She was about fifty-six, a hard worker, and loquacious. The third week she was with us, she said to me, "I bin lookin' at that pitcher on the mantelpiece. I hate bein' nosy, but is the lady's name by any chance MacIntosh, same as yours?"

I said yes, it was.

"I knew her, then," she said, nodding her moon face, smiling, oddly excited. "Each week I bin lookin' at her and thinkin' I know her from somewheres, but she looked too old. All that white hair. But she was from my hometown. Eileen MacIntosh. I used to pass down her street on my way to school. That's how I come to be familiar with her. We wasn't born on the same side of the tracks." She gave a bitter little chuckle. "You'd know all about her early days, I guess." She looked at me warily.

I tried not to lie. "I never knew her father. She seemed to think he was an almost perfect man."

She snorted. "Perfect, eh? Well there's perfect and perfect. And if called upon to describe himself, that's for sure the word he would have used. His family were from Nova Scotia a long ways back, and there's no one so proud nor so stubborn as a Nova Scotian. Everybody knows that. And that's what the MacIntoshes was."

"MacGregors," I said.

She looked at me for a moment, and then produced a smile that was spare and smug. "No," she said, "MacIntoshes." And then went on. "He was as thin as a cadaver and as tall as tall. Head like a hawk and back like a poker. He walked like he knew for certain that his first cousin on his mother's side was the king of England. Like someone was back there holdin' his train off the dirty sidewalks of Saint John."

I sat very still, hands clasped together to keep them from moving. I was afraid of stopping this amazing flow of information.

She looked at me slyly. "Want me to wipe down them walls now, Mrs. MacIntosh?"

"No, no, Geneva. Everyone needs a little break, and we're both tired, I'm sure. Just sit a minute and rest. The walls can wait." I hobbled over to the counter. "Let me get you a cup of coffee. Sugar?" I had some coffee waiting in a thermos.

"Three lumps," she said. "No milk."

We sat with our coffee cups, like two strangers. Any questions from me, I felt, would look too curious. Heart hammering, I sipped and waited.

Geneva was clearly torn between her enjoyment of the suspense and her eagerness to tell her tale. She took a few sips of her coffee and said, with maddening slowness, "Very good coffee, Mrs. MacIntosh."

"I hope it's not too strong," I said, stirring and stirring.

Finally she spoke. "They kept her hid, y'know, after it happened. They said she went away to college, but we knew different. Because the boy was from our part of town. Still and all, we was amazed that she took up with him. All that beauty and high class, sneakin' out at night to go dancin' and drivin' and whatever"—and here she smirked—"with someone who had a round face and no taller 'n her. Mind, she was some tall. But he was reckless and fun, and everybody loved him; and I guess there wasn't much laughter and gaddin' about in that big house on Waterloo Street. You does some wild things when you're sixteen. It seems like you goes a little bit crazy for a time. If parents'd just sit back and let the fever pass over, oftentimes the madness'd just go away all by itself. But Mr. MacIntosh forbid her ever to so much as smile at Georgie. That's why all the pussyfootin' around after dark, I suppose."

"What about her mother?"

"Oh, her mother." Geneva sniffed. "Nice enough, I guess, and no snob like the old man. But no backbone. Whatever he said, that was th' law, and she never did stand up to him for one second. Obeyed him even when he wasn't around. I had all that from my cousin Josie that did the cleanin' there for a while. She said Mrs. MacIntosh did a lotta cryin' and sobbin' behind her bedroom door, 'specially during them first long bad months. But I bet that mother wasn't what anyone would call an ounce of help to her girl. If one of your parents is sad all the time and the other one mad, there isn't much to choose from if you're lookin' for comfort."

"Sad," I said.

"Yes, sirree." Geneva nodded. "She never left that house. We knew she wasn't in college because there was people who saw her pass by the window. If you're human and if you're young, you can't keep away from a window twenty-four hours a day. I seen her once myself toward the end of her time, face like an angel, because she was beautiful, y'know, and belly as round and big as an October pumpkin. And wistful in the face when she parted them curtains. And somethin' else, too. Angry."

She took a few swallows of coffee and delicately nibbled on a chocolate chip cookie, holding up the little finger of her small square hand. I waited, determined to say no more. Finally she put down her cup.

"The old man thought we was trash, and he woulda bin furious if he'd of known what we seen. We may of bin trash, but we wasn't blind. Nor was we deaf. There was times when you could hear that baby cryin' clear to the end of the block."

I was scarcely breathing. I put my cup and saucer on the end table; it rattled when I held it.

"But they wasn't there long," she continued. "After about a month, he musta shipped them both out, 'cause it was like she disappeared off the face of the earth. And sure as shootin' no one in that town ever saw her again. Not ever."

She put down her coffee and sighed, and was quiet for a few moments. Then: "Her father went around with his hawk head as high as ever and his back as straight, makin' like nothin' had ever happened in that house to bring him down to the level of the rest of us. His blood was all mixed up with ours inside that baby's veins. That must of been some hard for him to take. But you'd never of known it to look at him."

She got up abruptly. "I'm real sorry, Mrs. Mac-Intosh," she said, "but all of a sudden I feel awful dizzy and sick in the stomach or head or somethin'. I know I ain't done yet, but could I leave the rest of the work till Tuesday?"

She didn't wait for my answer, but put the vacuum and pail away, gathering up her coat and umbrella as quickly as she could.

At the door, I put my hand on her arm for a moment. "Geneva," I said, "I hope you'll be all right." We looked at one another for a long moment, and something passed between us. A kind of knowing. Then I broke the spell.

"I'd drive you home, but I'm expecting a visitor at twelve. I'm sorry."

She spoke once more. "From the picture, she looks for all the world like the old man. Still beautiful, though." She sighed again. "Don't look to me like she suffered much after all."

I just said, "Good-bye, Geneva." She turned without

another word, and left. She never came to work for me again. She sent another woman in her place.

I looked at Thomas at the end of the table that evening, rubbing his stomach, correcting the boys' table manners, delivering statements to me about bank policies. We were eating macaroni and cheese.

"This is something that my mother never served," he said, giving his plate a barely perceptible shove.

I looked at him and realized that the afternoon's revelations had not eased the prodding irritation that his arrogance always produced in me. For an hour or two that afternoon, Thomas had become something different to me. Even his mother had had new things to say as she looked out at me from the frame with her proud, unlovable face.

But here I was reacting to them both in the usual manner. I watched him as he reduced Harold to tears with sharp criticisms of his speech, his work habits, his posture. "MacIntoshes don't cry," Thomas said.

Ah, but they do, I thought. What's more, Thomas, you would benefit enormously from a few tears yourself. And I could bring that about with one sentence. I smiled as I composed the four necessary words.

"Why are you smiling, Alfreda?" Thomas asked, puzzled, uneasy.

A fine household, I thought, when one is startled by a smile.

"Just thinking," I said. "Just thinking." Ashamed, I said no more. I thought of a dozen reasons to forgive, to excuse, to pity, to hold my tongue.

Then Tosh spoke. He sat up straight and drew in his young chin in a familiar way. "Father," he said, "I'm getting extremely high marks in school. Is there no way you could send me to that private school—Rothesay, isn't it?—advertised in the *Gleaner*? I know it costs a lot, but we're an important family, and I'd be associating with my own kind." He gave a little cough. "There'd be a better chance to realize my intellectual and social potential. It's not like you're a common laborer or anything."

I set my fork down very carefully and looked at my son. He looked unfamiliar, new. He's twelve years old, I thought. I hope it's not too late. Fear touched the back of my neck. Thomas was nodding, pursing his lips, patting, scratching, dabbing at his macaroni and cheese, looking with favor on his elder son.

It was not my intention to be cruel. After all, there were ways in which Thomas might find it a relief to know what I knew. I bought a miniature teddy bear the next day and put it on his desk beside his calendar.

"Where did this come from?" he asked, after dinner.

"From me," I said. "It's a present."

"What an odd idea," he said, but he picked it up and stroked the fur with his index finger. Then he replaced it, changing its position several times, standing back to look at the effect.

I waited until after the national news. Then I brought him his favorite peppermint tea, brewed in the silver teapot, our wedding present from his mother.

"Thomas," I said, touching him gently on the shoulder. "If you have a moment, there are a few rather important things I'd like to discuss with you."

The House on High Street

WHEN VIRGINIA WAS in her midforties, she started thinking about the past—her own past. Up until then, she'd just moved from one part of her life to the next, without looking back very much. But then, all of a sudden, without any real warning, she started to care about those things in her life that were finished. She didn't know why this happened. It just did. Maybe there was a part of her that began to suspect that nothing is ever finished. Perhaps she watched her two children and started to wonder about her own childhood. Or possibly she could feel herself sliding downhill in the direction of old age and felt that someday she might need some memories to explain who she was and where she had come from.

One day, she sat down for a second cup of coffee after Jeff and the girls had left for work and school. She loved this part of the day. The early morning confusion was over—the mislaid pencils and notebooks, the lost car keys, the nagging over breakfast choices, the general air of flight—and the rest of her work had not yet begun. She looked out the kitchen window at the bright May morning and thought, This is the kind of weather that Mum always chose for our annual trip to Dartmouth. She always said it was a pity to waste a ferry ride on a rainstorm. And why go in the winter, when it's too cold to enjoy the outer deck? No. She'd look out the window on a morning such as this and announce, "This is the day. It's fine, and it's Saturday, and it's time we went." Nobody needed to ask her what she meant. They knew. They were going to Dartmouth to see the old aunts and uncles. In the house on High Street. Virginia's father was spared. On the day she was now remembering, he went off to collect his fishing gear, well satisfied with this turn of events. But Virginia and her brother always joined their mother on this particular expedition. "Hurry!" she said. They rushed upstairs to change into their very best clothes.

Virginia is up in her bedroom looking in her closet, trying to choose between her two Sunday dresses. "Your blue velvet with the collar," her mother calls out. "That's the one to wear. They haven't seen you in it yet." Good. She always loves wearing it. It is a deep rich blue, and the collar is made of white lace. Her hair is long and straight and blond, and she knows that she looks pretty in this dress. She doesn't put that thought into so many words, but when she has finished dressing and looks in the mirror beside her pink bureau, she likes what she sees smiling back at her from the glass. She wears long beige stockings, held up by garters from her white cotton vest— called a *waist*. The stockings itch the back of her knees, but she's allowed to wear her patent leather shoes with the straps. This makes up for the itching. It is 1936.

Her brother, Ian, is looking less pleased. He doesn't like dressing up, and he's feeling uncomfortable and silly in his stiff clean clothes. He has a lot of curly blond hair, and he's thinking that in the fancy shirt he's wearing, he looks like a girl. He hates that.

Ian is ten years old. Later on, Virginia will remember his age, because this is the month when Freckles O'Brien will die of polio. None of his friends will ever forget that time. They will fix events according to whether they happened before or after Freckles's death. In that year, they are not grieving for Freckles so much as they are agitating over their own mortality. They become hypochondriacs for a while, fearful of germs, aware of what a headache may signify, their minds cluttered by visions of wheelchairs and braces. Infantile paralysis, they call it. Not polio.

If Ian is ten, then Virginia must be eight. She loves going to visit the aunts and uncles. She enjoys their eccentricities and their flaws. And when they return home, she will take pleasure in her mother's spirited account of the day to her father. Virginia's eyes are always wide open, watching, and yes, her ears are flapping.

The ferry ride is, as always, wonderful. They park the car in the vehicle lanes and then climb the steps to the middle deck, from which they watch their departure. The breeze is cool, and Virginia sits down on one of the benches close to her mother, hugging her coat around her. Ian wanders all over the boat, inspecting things— the life preservers, the wheelhouse, the tangle of mysterious machinery.

Some Dartmouthians ride on the ferry every day, but for most Haligonians, a ferry ride is a major adventure. Huge gulls are riding the wind, far up in the sky, and fat little tugboats are chugging down the harbor toward George's Island. The water seems to be full of vessels— large and small ones—and Virginia marvels that they do not bump into one another. Then she remembers that once, nineteen years ago, two ships did precisely that. And the collision and resulting explosion wiped out one-third of the city of Halifax, as well as inflicting terrible destruction on Dartmouth. What would it have been like to be on the ferry that day? She shivers, and pulls her coat even more tightly around her.

"Cold?" her mother asks.

"No," she says. "Just thinking."

When they drive off the ferry and start their journey to the house on High Street, Virginia starts contemplating about what lies ahead. She imagines the aunts and uncles standing at the doorway, ready to greet them—old, deaf, and very interesting. The house will loom up above her like a storybook mansion, its eaves and verandas trimmed with a profusion of Victorian carvings and curlicues, its yellow paint shining in the sun. From the front lawn they will be able to see right out to sea, past the islands and all the way to the horizon.

It is almost exactly as she has imagined it. As the car rolls into the circular driveway, the heavy front door opens and the four of them are standing there, their hearing aids sprouting wires that connect to the round amplifiers decorating three of their chests. They are shouting at one another and at their visitors; the air is alive with voices, warm with smiles. Virginia is so delighted to watch all this that she forgets to check the horizon for ships.

When she enters the front hall, she is once again

dazzled by its size and contents. Each year it is both familiar and surprising to her. The gleaming surface of the mahogany staircase rises in front of them, and a dark red carpet marches up to the second floor, held down by polished brass rods. A lamp on the newel post is lit, although it is ten o'clock on a sunny morning. The rose-colored glass shade is held up by four scantily clad young maidens, made of some kind of dull metal. The drapery that they are wearing covers most of the embarrassing places, but its arrangement looks loose and precarious. One of the metal maidens has a bare breast. Virginia looks at it very carefully and thinks that she'd like to touch it. Will it be round like her mother's or pointy like Aunt Gloria's? It's a bit too high up for her to be sure. Virginia is not an authority on breasts, having seen her mother and Aunt Gloria naked only once—in one of the little unpainted bathing houses on Hubbards Beach.

Aunt Melissa is short and stout, but very erect and puffed up. She has wiry white hair and an unbeautiful face, dominated by an overlarge nose. It is clear that she is in charge, so it would appear that nothing has changed. She is telling everyone where to go—into the parlor— and she is ringing a little silver bell, ringing and ringing, to summon the maid with the tea. Virginia sits down carefully on one of the brocaded chairs, secretly running her fingers over its silken surface. All around her are precious and exotic things—especially the brass clock on the marble mantel, whose pendulum turns and then turns again, with a lazy and mesmerizing movement. She looks at the Dresden figurines, the ornate silver candlesticks, the fringed lamp, the lace curtains, the velvet pincushion, the carved wooden footstool. She loves and she covets almost everything she sees. The room smells of deeply embedded dust and stale face powder. Ian looks uncomfortable and unhappy, but Virginia feels no pity for him.

Aunt Melissa's husband is Uncle Hal, and Virginia likes him the best of all. He is tall and uncoordinated, bumping into things, tripping over the edges of scatter rugs. She remembers this about him, so she watches him carefully, noting that he's still doing it, still bumbling around. However, he is the only one of the four who hears at all well. He seems a gentle and kindly person, and finds a stereoscopic machine for Ian to look through at a set of three-dimensional pictures. Although Virginia does not care whether or not Ian is happy, she admires Uncle Hal's sensitive hospitality. He obeys all of Aunt Melissa's shouted instructions ("Get Ida a more comfortable chair, Hal!" and "Go tell Minnie to hurry up with the tea!" and "Stop fidgeting, Hal!"). But mostly he just stands in front of the fireplace as though warming the seat of his pants, smiling at the three visitors, shifting his weight from one long leg to the other.

Virginia wonders who owns the house. If it belongs to Aunt Melissa and Uncle Hal, why do Aunt Melissa's sisters and brother live here, too? This seems odd to her, but intriguing. Or maybe it belongs to the family, to the MacIsaacs; if so, it is Uncle Hal who is the hanger-on, the person who doesn't quite fit. Virginia feels a vague pity for him, perhaps because he is the only one who is quiet. The others are all shouting at one another.

The sister and brother here are Auntie Hester and Uncle Sherman. Auntie Hester is small and mousy and solemn, her gray hair drawn back from her face in a scraggly little bun. But her features are regular and firm, and Virginia decides that she may have been very pretty when she was young and didn't have all those lines in her face. She is not married. Once Virginia asked her mother about this, and she said, "She was in love once, long ago, but it didn't work out." Virginia looks upon her as a tragic figure, like a princess in a fairy tale who has been thwarted in love. As Auntie Hester moves about obeying Aunt Melissa's various commands, two tendrils of curly hair come loose from her severe hair arrangement and lie along each temple. With that sudden softness, her old face reveals what must have been there forty-five years ago. She is slender and graceful in her simple navy blue dress, and wears a velvet band around her wrinkled neck.

Uncle Sherman is red-faced and blustery, full of loud pronouncements—on the weather ("This will be a long, hot summer, mark my words!"), women ("They're far too full of themselves, nowadays!"), politics ("Anyone's crazy who votes for the Liberal Party. Damn Grits!"). His wife is in a sanitorium with TB and has been there for over thirty years.

The tea is wheeled in on a tea wagon by Minnie, starched and stiff in a black-and-white uniform. It is passed around in delicate china cups, one of which has butterfly wings for a handle. Virginia's desire to own this cup is almost physical in its intensity. She and Ian get milk, in small manageable glasses. They're careful to set them down on the coasters provided. There are three plates of assorted small cakes, arranged on a three-tiered silver contraption, and Ian perks up a bit during this part of the visit.

On the whole, much is said, and little is listened to. Maybe, Virginia thinks, this is because no one can hear properly. Or perhaps for other reasons. However, she is an avid listener. She hears everything, and tucks it all away for future consideration. Sitting there on the embroidered chair, she categorizes her aunts and uncles. Aunt Melissa—the bossy one; Uncle Hal—the sweet one; Auntie Hester—the sad one; Uncle Sherman—the angry one.

Once Virginia asked her mother what they all did with their time when the three of them weren't around to be entertained. What did they do with the three hundred and sixty-four other days in the year?

"They play bridge," she said. "And scream at one another."

"Because they can't hear?"

"Well, yes. And also because they all have terrible tempers. All the MacIsaacs, that is. Auntie Hester looks so meek and mild, but when she plays bridge something comes over her. Mostly she just *looks,* but if you got in the way of that look, it could kill you." She laughed. "Heaven help anyone who plays the wrong trick. I'd rather put my head in a noose than play bridge with that bunch."

"If they're so cranky, why do you visit them?"

"They're family."

"How did they get to be family?" Virginia pressed, not understanding her reply.

"They're my father's brother and sisters."

"Did he have temper tantrums, too?"

"Yes."

"Was he deaf, too?"

"Yes."

"Will you get to be deaf sometime, too? And bad-tempered?"

Her mother paused. Finally, she said, "I had a mother as well as a father. I'm not entirely locked in by my genes."

Virginia couldn't tuck that one away in her head. She didn't understand any of it.

When Minnie comes in to clear away the tea things, Virginia knows that the time has come. They will go upstairs now and visit Aunt Adelaide. They will also go to see Benjamin. Virginia has been looking forward to this ever since she changed into her blue velvet dress. But now that the moment is at hand, she can feel a familiar hollow sensation in her chest, a confusing combination of delight and dread.

They visit Aunt Adelaide first. Her sisters and brother are very hard of hearing, but Aunt Adelaide is stone-deaf. Virginia tries to imagine a life of total silence, but her imagination cannot take her that far. Aunt Adelaide is also arthritic to a degree that Virginia has never witnessed in any other person. Her hands are misshapen and fixed, as solid as a statue's. All of her that is visible—her face, her fingers, the skinny ankle that can be seen below her afghan—looks like a wax doll. She can move almost nothing, but she can manage to flip over a page. She reads and sleeps. That is all. Virginia's mind is agape with fascination and horror. Auntie Hester is the one who looks after Aunt Adelaide, the one who bathes her, brings her books from Miss Bell's lending library in Dartmouth, feeds her, does all the necessary bathroom things. Virginia tries not to think about the details.

Aunt Melissa writes Aunt Adelaide a note. "Here are Ida and Ian and Virginia."

Aunt Adelaide offers a stiff and toothless smile; her eyes are glassy bright.

"Hello," Virginia's mother writes. "How lovely to see you."

More notes pass back and forth, and Aunt Adelaide manages a shallow nod, smiles, and speaks in a high, strained voice—barely audible, and to Virginia, unintelligible. She has on a frilly white nightgown and a mauve shawl protects her narrow shoulders. Auntie Hester must have dressed her like a doll, thinks Virginia, lifting each rigid arm and then setting it down again. An afghan covers all the rest of her—except for that waxy ankle that protrudes indecently above the woolly slipper. Virginia does not take her eyes off her for one instant. She can hear Ian's heavy breathing behind her.

Next they go to see Benjamin. Auntie Hester and Uncle Hal don't stay around for this version of show-and-tell. Benjamin is Aunt Melissa and Uncle Hal's son, their only child. Virginia does not know what is wrong with him. He is a fully grown person, but he is lying curled up on his side, with the sheet pulled up over his shoulder. Virginia can see that his neck is long and thin and very white. If you look carefully, you discover that he is tied to the bed by a very long cloth strap fastened to the bedsprings. He has handsome features, but it is hard to decide how old he is. Maybe thirty-five years old. Perhaps forty-five. But he looks much younger. His eyes are open, but he is focusing on nothing. Everyone speaks to him, Aunt Melissa and Uncle Sherman shouting, Virginia's mother speaking quietly, but they all know he cannot understand any of it and that he will not reply.

Benjamin frightens Virginia, but he also interests her enormously. She doesn't know where the fear comes from, but it is real and she feels it deeply. She believes that if Benjamin suddenly looked up at one of them and

said, "Hello," she'd have nightmares about it for the rest
of her life.

One day, about a year after this visit, Virginia gathered
up the courage to ask her mother why Benjamin was the
way he was. Her mother didn't answer right away, but
apparently she decided that Virginia was old enough to
know, because she told her.

"When he was born he was perfectly normal," she
said. "Or so I'm told. I never saw him when he was an
infant. Uncle Hal had a position in Bermuda for a while.
That's where Benjamin was born. It was in Bermuda that
they all started living together. They thought it might
cure Uncle Sherman's wife, but it didn't."

"But what about Benjamin?" prompted Virginia.

"Oh yes. Well. They all came back when Benjamin
was about ten months old. One day when Aunt Melissa
was carrying him into the garden, she dropped him on
the flagstone path. She must have tripped or something.
He's been like that ever since." She frowned. "What a
tragedy for Aunt Melissa and Uncle Hal," she said. "All
those years."

But on this day, Virginia doesn't know any of those interesting details. Benjamin is a mystery, and she wants to

watch him a little longer. When Aunt Melissa and Uncle Sherman are outside showing them the garden, she slips away and reenters the house by the back door.

Climbing up the mahogany staircase on the silent carpet, she pauses in the little alcove at the top of the landing. She can hear Auntie Hester and Uncle Hal talking, and she doesn't want them to know that she's up here being nosy. She peeks around to see where they are. Their backs are to her, and they are standing in the doorway of Benjamin's room. Uncle Hal's arm is around Auntie Hester's shoulder. She is standing very close to him, touching him with the whole left side of her body. She says, "He was such a beautiful baby."

Uncle Hal looks down at her and smooths a strand of hair away from her forehead. "And still is," he says. He speaks very quietly, and she cannot hear him. She's as deaf as the rest of them.

"Ours," says Auntie Hester. She whispers this, but she spits the word out, and Virginia can hear her very clearly. Auntie Hester leaves Uncle Hal and goes into the room, adjusting the covers, smoothing the sheets over Benjamin's humped-up body, tucking him in. Then she touches him gently on the side of his face.

When she turns to leave the room, her face reveals a mixture of grief and rage, terrible in its intensity. Virginia hears again her mother's words: *If you got in the way of that look, it could kill you.* But Virginia is not in the way, nor is Uncle Hal.

When Auntie Hester reaches him, he looks down at her for a long time. Then, as Virginia looks on in amazement, he kisses Auntie Hester upon the lips.

Virginia once saw the girl next door when she returned home with her boyfriend after a dance. They stood on her veranda in the full glare of the outdoor light, and kissed. The kiss lasted for such a long time that when they did it again, Virginia counted, "One-and, two-and, three-and . . ." She got to thirty-five before they drew away from one another.

When Auntie Hester and Uncle Hal kiss, it isn't just a friendly peck. No. It's exactly like the kiss of the girl next door and her boyfriend. Virginia finds herself counting. She reaches thirteen, and then they stop.

Virginia's astonishment makes her feel vacant and weak. Her legs are like chunks of putty, but she tiptoes across the landing to the back stairs and goes down quietly. Her head is so full of questions that she needs to find some place where she can be alone, in order to think about the answers. She lets herself out the side door and goes to sit in a small gazebo at the edge of the garden. Virginia stays there in the little summerhouse for a long time.

Virginia looked down at the table and saw that her coffee had not been touched. The cup was cold. But outside, the morning was still bright and the air very clear. Through the trees and beyond the grain elevators, she could glimpse the intense blue of Halifax Harbor.

"Yes," she said, speaking aloud in the empty room. "We always went on a day exactly like this one."

But no wonder Virginia remembered that year so clearly. Freckles and his death. Benjamin and his life.

Birds, Horses, and Muffins

THE MORNING IS BRIGHT and sunny, the sea a startling blue. As the plane approaches Halifax, I wonder once again about the wisdom of attending this reunion. A great deal of time has passed. Memories are shifting around in my mind, nudging me forward, pulling me back. But I found myself free to come; the time seemed right. Besides, I've always been a person with a lot of curiosity.

As we circle the airport area, everything is as I remember it—the dense forest, the sprinkling of wooden houses, the network of lakes, and to the south and east, the endless stretch of ocean. I take a long breath and sink deeper into the seat. This is the landscape that once gave me such peace and comfort when it was needed. After forty years away, it is clear to me that this is still my home.

My home of another kind, my family home, generates less peaceful memories. My mother and father have been dead for many years, and Wayne, my brother, moved away to Vancouver as soon as he could decently leave home. But my sister, Ardith—pretty Ardith, confident Ardith—still lives in Nova Scotia. She of the helpless laughter, the storybook romances, the untroubled mind.

I move restlessly against my seat belt and admit to feeling guilty about that last thought. I realize I'm being unfair, and heaven knows I've been on the side of justice and reason for most of my life. I must try to concentrate on ways in which things have not always been easy for Ardith. Otherwise I will fall into the old trap of not liking her.

She did have those difficulties when her daughter was going through her nymphomaniac phase. She wrote me about that. And there were the bad times she had with Joey—her middle son—during·what she referred to as "the turbulent teens." She used to say those words with an indulgent smile. Exactly the way she would smile, hands folded in her lap or fondling her gin and tonic, while Joey—aged six—was *biting the leg* of that shy Millicent O'Grady. While Ardith said nothing—except sometimes, "Boys will be boys," or "Too young to know better." But he wasn't all that young, and he did an awful lot of biting. While Millicent's poor mother looked as though she were going to burst wide open. Grabbed her own glass so tightly one day that it actually shattered in her grasp. They took her to the hospital, where they put ten stitches in the palm of her right hand.

"Now what on earth," said Ardith to me that evening, "would make a thing like that happen?" The composition of the glass was probably what she had in mind.

What did I answer? Nothing. I experienced the same helpless sadness that I used to feel when Mother would get us ready for birthday parties—Ardith and me. Ardith would be wearing a dress with frills or lace, and maybe even an eyelet petticoat showing itself ever so slightly beneath the full skirt. My own dress would be simple and unadorned, probably navy blue with white piping around the Peter Pan collar. Something that wouldn't look too ridiculous on my lanky body, with its bony knees, its long unlovely face. "You have to dress them in what suits them," I'd heard my mother boast to Mrs. Eaton, on whom she unloaded all her complaints and opinions.

Once, before I knew better than to try to upset the system, I said to my mother, as we stood surveying the rack of little girls' dresses in Simpson's, "Mummy, I'd like to have a dress like Ardith's." To which she replied, "Oh, come now, Aggie." But she must have seen the hunger in my eyes, and she was not by nature or intent a cruel woman. She slid the pink dress off the hanger, the dress I'd been fingering—caressing the stiff organdy flounce, the wide frothy skirt. Frowning, she held it up in front of me in order to get a vague idea of what it would look like on me. Apparently the vague idea was all she needed. "No," she said, and put it back on the hanger. "It wouldn't look well on you at all."

She was probably right. Looking back over a distance of seventy years and with a lifetime of dresses behind me, I can even see that my clothes had a certain subdued class, whereas Ardith's were a trace vulgar in their profuse femininity, their crass prettiness. But is taste always more important than the kind of hot desires felt by children? Is it valuable for a child to spend so much of his or her life feeling unsatisfied? Maybe a few of those frilly dresses— even just one—would have driven the lust for frills out of my system. As it is, at the age of seventy-six, growing more angular with each passing day, I can still long for a ruffle at the neck or sleeve, some sort of sweet excess to compensate for all those years of tasteful simplicity. "You're just not the type," Mother would say to me, giving me a little hug to show that she loved me in spite of that fact. She hugged Ardith *because* of things.

Well then, I used to ask myself, just what type am I, anyway? When I was fifteen, I found out. One day, Ardith came home from school with a new game. She was fourteen, and many of her statements or announcements were preceded by shrieks of high-pitched laughter. She came bursting in the back door and yelled, "Guess what?"

"What?" we all asked—Mum, Dad, Wayne, and me.

Then came the wild mirth and shrill guffaws. "Ellen Jamieson says," she gasped, between hiccups of joy, "that everyone is either a bird, a horse, or a muffin."

"What?" exclaimed my mother, puzzled.

"Think about it," choked Ardith. "Take Marybelle Rogers. Marybelle is obviously a muffin—probably a bran muffin, at that." More hoots of laughter.

"And you, Mom," she said, "you're a bird. Quick, small, flitting around."

"I get it! I get it!" laughed Wayne, seventeen, and usually above or beyond our young and female foolishness. "And there are lots of kinds of birds—ducks, owls, eagles, sparrows. Mom's a sparrow. And that guy who sells the papers on Barrington Street—he's a partridge."

"Right!" Ardith was hugging herself to keep the laughter from spilling out again. "And lots of kinds of muffins. Little, round, cute blueberry muffins. Or big, doughy corn muffins. Oh my gosh!" And the giggles exploded again. "Miss Cosmos, our math teacher, is a corn muffin!"

"And I suppose you're a bird, too, Ardith," said my mother, catching on.

"I guess so," laughed Ardith. "Sally Epstein said I was a canary. Yellow hair and lots of singing," she said.

"And you—" Ardith swung around and looked me full in the face.

There was a silence. No one spoke for what seemed to me a very long time. From across the room, I was staring at my own face in the mirror above the sink. Wayne coughed. Ardith left her unfinished sentence hovering in the air.

My mother's voice cut into the awful stillness. "Go on upstairs, the three of you, and wash up before supper."

As I left the kitchen, I looked at my father with distaste. Another horse. This is what heredity does to you. On him, it looked good. At fifty years old, there he was—a large, handsome, prizewinning horse, long in the jaw, distinguished, with a still-impressive mane. Wayne, too—a graceful, long-legged thoroughbred, winner of races. But I was a girl. What was my mother doing with her genes the night I was conceived? I was neither blind nor stupid. I could see that face in the mirror. It wasn't even a pony—playful and charming. Or a heartwarming colt, engaging, large-eyed, full of promise. No. That face was just plain horse. A lifetime of oats stretched ahead of me.

By the age of seventeen, I had pretty much given up hope that my body would eventually compensate for my unfortunate face. If, at that age, you are long of limb and built more or less straight, the chances are good that you'll remain that way forever. And I was right to think that. No deep cleavage ever diverted attention from my mouthful of overlarge teeth. Nor had I hips to swing or even a tiny waist to cinch in with those wide belts that we would wear above our circular skirts, ten years later, when the New Look sailed in, with its Gibson girl bows and blouses.

The Second World War, by that time, had come and gone, and for me it had borne no fruit. It was almost impossible not to be fêted and dated in wartime Halifax—a truly happy hunting ground for most girls. For six years, the city overflowed with lonely and vulnerable young servicemen, crazed for female companionship. But not *that* crazed. I can tell you that much from firsthand experience. A handsome man can be very wonderful to look at, but (regardless of how you may feel about war) a handsome man in a uniform is one of life's most dazzling spectacles. Observing the rolling gait of the naval ratings as they cruised along Barrington Street four abreast, their bell-bottom trousers tight over their slim hips; gazing at army officers, their brass buttons shining, their postures proud, erect, as they saluted one another on the dizzy slant of Sackville Street; stealing glimpses of air-force blue, tangling with a dirndl skirt among the bushes of Point Pleasant Park: seeing such things, daily, made my chest tight with dreams. But sightings, watchings, and steamy imaginings were all I could hope for. I learned this very early. There was something very insulting about the way those young men looked at me. They didn't look with loathing. Their eyes simply grazed my face and bounced off again with such speed that there was scarcely enough time to feel wounded.

But wounded I most certainly was. I used to regard the men around me as if they were rare and exotic tropical flowers. I longed to touch them, to smell them, to keep them in my bedroom. My passions were fiery hot, frequent, unrequited. At night, I writhed upon my bed in an agony of frustration, or read sexy novels, hour after sleepless hour. I was in love a dozen times a year. When I was beside myself with longing, I would often go down and sit on the little beach at the foot of South Street, drawing comfort from the Northwest Arm, the Fleming Tower, the gulls, the quiet, the absence of people. I would sit on a favorite flat rock, propped up by a tree, reading, watching the lazy ducks, shutting my eyes against the western light, gathering peace from the warmth of the sun and the sounds of the incoming tide. On that beach, I came to recognize who I really was.

Well—my brain was good. The more fervent feminists of today would inform me, I am sure (were I to ask), that this is all a woman ought to need. That and her heaven-sent female intuition. But if you yearn for male companionship and the comfort and pleasure of children, brains are often not enough to deliver up those prizes—not even today, I warrant, although the women's movement has taken us a great deal further in that direction. The curly headed beauties\who want to be loved for their brains alone have a worthy aim. Those of us who have never been loved at all could cash in very nicely should they ever achieve it.

It was shortly before war broke out that I took my brains to university, and I was a highly successful student. My transcript is a dazzling array of straight A's. I was even moderately content. The girls liked me, and I them. The professors thought I was a marvel. Because my family moved away to another city, I stayed in residence. There

I had a number of very close friends, particularly Pamela Jansen, with whom I spent long hours discussing Truth, Politics, God, Original Sin. When there was a dance, I was there to pin the corsages on the dresses before the girls left for the gym in a flurry of haste and laughter. This was not a function I enjoyed.

I tried to ignore the fact that my high grades alienated me still further from the young men whose attentions I so urgently craved. But I refused to be a traitor to my brains. I loved the library, the smell of the books in the stacks, the little desks in the carrels, the intense stillness of the place. Researching essays delighted me. I enjoyed taking exams. These were my secrets. I told no one.

Eventually, I lost touch with every one of the girls with whom I shared the second floor of Shirreff Hall. Fond though I was of them, I wearied of the incessant chatter about their boyfriends, their daring and forbidden sexual exploits (pretty tame, I must say, by today's standards), their whispered confidences about what was said and done in the storied alcoves of the residence. However, tired of it or not, I persevered for a long time; they were, after all, my friends. I sat, half-crazed with boredom, through a score of bridal showers, hearing the verses read aloud from the cards, watching the colored bows accumulate, listening to the murmurs of delight, looking with a certain detached envy at the mountains of gifts—stemware, fat, woolly bath towels, sets of woven placemats, pieces of delicate bone china—things one would never think of buying for oneself.

But when the babies started to come, I drew the line. I saw my friends through morning sickness, bulging bellies, accounts of their prolonged labors. That I could manage. However, when the babies actually materialized, when diapers and Pablum and breastfeeding and something called sleeping-through-the-night became the chief topics of conversation, I retreated from the scene. Besides, the real live babies disturbed me. My desire for the woolly bath towels could be a disconnected experience. Those babies reached into a soft and vulnerable part of me, inflicting a pain I could not tolerate. No. I could not. Their plump little legs and tiny toes. Their round faces with their toothless smiles. The sweet-and-sour smell of their sturdy bodies. Pamela Jansen gradually accumulated five of them and became too busy mothering to talk about Truth or Politics.

Finally, I could not cope with all that watching and not having. That's when I moved away. I took the first job that Toronto offered me. I left behind my friends and family, the sea that had comforted and nourished me, a landscape that was a compelling part of my beginnings.

Tucking my Ph.D. and my law degree in my briefcase, I went forth into the worlds of law and politics, making my mark upon them—not as deep a mark as I could have made today, but nonetheless a very significant dent. I chaired committees, supervised a small army of employees, dined with premiers and presidents, was interviewed on national TV, traveled executive class, owned a penthouse in Toronto. I drove a Mercedes, shopped at Creed's, kept two Siamese cats. My biological clock ticked away its time, and my reproductive system came and went without even one fleeting seduction to disturb its slumber. Godmother to many children, I never held my own. While other women complained of sexual harassment, this had never been, for me, a problem. But I had a large corner office with a spectacular view of Lake Ontario. Original paintings hung upon the walls. Light gray broadloom covered the floor from side to side. Through the doors of that office, exceedingly interesting people came and went. I became an enormously successful woman. A successful person. And a happy one.

After a day of revisiting old and familiar places—the ocean side of Point Pleasant Park, the Public Gardens, the ramparts of the Citadel, Fleming Tower with its giddy staircase, my beach on South Street—I am back at the hotel, dressing for the first event of the class reunion, the only reunion I have ever attended. Tonight, there is to be a large cocktail party for all the groups. I have chosen to wear a white blouse with a softly ruffled neck, a gray-blue Chanel jacket and a matching gathered skirt. The outfit is very expensive, very chic, including—much to my surprise—the blouse with its ruffled neckline. Those ruffles are softening something in my austere face. Briefly, I regret that my mother failed to recognize that possibility.

I have done all I can to ready myself for this occasion, but as I fasten my earrings, I notice that my hands are shaking. I discover that my thirty-five years in positions of power in the worlds of law and politics have not prepared me for this event. I am nineteen years old again—hesitant, inadequate, haunted by almost forgotten complexes. I am full of fear, and ask myself what I will find to say to all those people with whom I shared my youth. I wonder, in fact, who I actually was, way back then.

I have contacted none of my former classmates—nor have I phoned Ardith, who had followed me to college a year after I began—so no one accompanies me to the Student Union Building. I enter the large reception room entirely alone. I look around. This is an occasion that spans all the classes—from the '30s to the '90s. Many young people are in attendance. I ignore them. I scan the side of the room where the older people are gathered. There, in fact, is Ardith, whom I have not seen for seventeen years. Viewing her from this distance, I am able to study her almost objectively, unimpeded by seventy-five years of knowing. She looks cheerful. She sounds shrill, although I am too far away to hear her conversation. Not changed, I think, as I draw closer. But look again. She is short, stuffed looking. A muffin, to be exact. Her hair is thinning, and I can see patches of pink scalp under the white curls. Her dress is navy blue, straight cut, no doubt to minimize her considerable girth. It has touches of white at the neck, on the sleeves, and an army of pearl buttons marches down the center of her enormous bosom.

I look over the rest of the geriatric scene. I see a lot of bald heads and fat paunches among men who are unrecognizable, but whom I may have hungered for in days gone by. A scattering few of the men remain more or less intact, marginally attractive, still in possession of their hair, almost erect. But most of them look frail. There is a preponderance of women. I think about birth and death statistics, and realize that many of the heroes of my youth are probably lingering on in nursing homes, babbling, clutching stuffed animals, drooling a little onto their white bibs.

A few couples stand uneasily on the sidelines, attempting animated conversation, husband with wife, wife with husband—couples who have been speaking together for fifty years, trying now to think of something new to say, so that onlookers won't realize how uncomfortable, how lonely they feel. The ones who know one another are grouped according to their sex, the men standing up, but usually clutching something—the back of a chair, the edge of a bookcase—talking man talk. Cars, taxes, fishing, golf, prostates, the deficit. The women are all sitting down in a group, over on the south side of the enormous room, huddled around the low table of chips and nuts and dips, talking woman talk. Grandchildren, arthritis, recipes for perfect meringues, condoms in high school rest rooms (this topic delivered in whispers), hysterectomies, Florida.

I survey this scene, catching snippets of conversation, and struggle to connect those tired and wrinkled faces to the people with whom I may have drunk coffee or played tennis. I do see one face that I can still name, and I feel a leap of recognition and delight. It's Pamela Jansen. Although greatly changed, I can see as I watch her talking, gesticulating, laughing, that she is still the same person. Maybe we can go off in a corner somewhere and talk about Original Sin. There, over by the window, is Jim Atkins. He was always kind to me. And I'm sure I'm looking at Whatsisname, the president of the senior class, looking gray of skin and limp. I am visited by thoughts of decay, time, forgiveness, the roundness of life—the feeling of having come full circle to a place I have nonetheless never visited before.

I approach the group with confidence, head high. I do not ask myself why this is so. There are reasons one might offer. Now, in my seventy-sixth year, I look as attractive as they do—better than most. This is certainly a factor. My skin—even on my gaunt face—is firm, and my body slender. There is no longer any need to bend to their physical power. I tell myself—possibly unjustly—that most of them are locked into a middle-class cage, holding fast to their clothes, their food, their families, their narrow opinions. I am at home with judges and mandarins, diplomats and tycoons, artists and symphony conductors. I am urgently concerned about the needs and rights of women and Native peoples and blacks—and of other more poorly represented people—the ugly, the shy, the frightened.

But these are not the chief reasons why I approach the group with confidence, yes, and with pleasure. I am suddenly comfortable in this place because I know that everything passes, nothing is ever permanent, even pain. I see death in front of me, and faced with death, everything else looks simple, manageable.

But it is not my sister and my old friends whom I greet first. Instead, I stop for a while with one of the couples who are hovering so nervously on the outskirts of the main group. "Hello," I say. "Maybe you don't remember me. I'm Agatha Donahoe, class of forty. I've been away."

The Diary

Here it is, then. You said on Friday that if I found it impossible to talk about it, I should try to write it all down. You suggested that it was a good way to start the New Year—like a resolution—something new and changing. You told me not to worry about grammar or sentence structure, but just to let it all pour out like a boil releasing its poisons. Its *pus,* in fact—your word, not mine. This is not easy for me. Releasing anything, that is. Or, to tell you the truth, to write anything without checking to make sure it is correct, without erasing any mistakes or signs of carelessness. My father said that anything worth doing was worth doing well. Nonetheless, I will try. Fortunately, you also said that I don't have to show the diary to you. I don't expect that I will. I can't bear the kind of disloyalty that washes family linen, soiled or otherwise, in public and to strangers. Although of course you are not really a stranger. But you know what I mean.

And I'm here alone. No one can see what I'm saying or how I'm saying it. But that's the crazy part. Even when I'm alone, maybe especially when I'm alone, I sit in judgment upon myself. I am my own judge and jailer. Probably that's hackneyed; it may even be a quote. But I'm going to try not to worry about that sort of thing. This is a diary, not a piece of literature.

I am fifty-five years old. I am married to a businessman who is successful and scrupulously honest. His name is Meredith Wentworth. I feel that the name has weight and dignity. He usually treats me with respect and with decency. We have two sons, both of them in their twenties. Their names are Gerald and Luther. They have always been well behaved and courteous, and they are now employed in their father's business. I have no daughters. Some people say that this is unfortunate, but I don't mind at all, because you never really miss something you have never had.

Tonight the boys are coming to dinner with their girlfriends. I must put the turkey in the oven before too long. Gerald's girl wears too much makeup; her clothes are invariably too tight, and her name is Samantha. Can you believe such a name? I've often seen them together downtown, but this is the first time he has brought her home. When they are together, they touch one another far too much. This worries me. Meredith is almost certain to disapprove. And she is not Luther's type either. His girl's name is Jane, and she is everything a parent could hope for in a daughter-in-law. I am hoping against hope that they will marry.

January 3

I didn't write yesterday because I was too tired. You said I was not to force it, although you also advised me to write *something* each day, even if it was just to say how I felt.

I feel terrible.

That's mainly because of New Year's dinner. But that's not primarily what you want me to write about. You said to try to write about my childhood. All right. The least I can do, I suppose, is to make an effort.

When I think back to my childhood, the first image I see is my father. He was enormous. Or at least so he seemed. In snapshots, he appears to be about the same height as other men, but even with that visual evidence before me, I find this hard to believe. He was very dark, with a black beard—in the days before anyone had a beard, except possibly one's grandfather. He wore thick glasses, and his eyes were very fixed and piercing behind them. He was a Presbyterian minister. I can see him up there, huge and erect in his black robes, lifted far above us by his pulpit and by his purpose. His voice was deep and powerful and very compelling.

"The wages of sin is death!" he would boom down at us from on high. With his voice, his bearing, it was easy to believe him. Then the hymns would follow, militantly urging virtue or melodiously promising peace and joy to the sinless. I believed everything he said. It was not hard to do this. After all, he was my father. Besides, he looked exactly like God.

New Year's dinner was just dreadful. Samantha's neckline was so low that you could see the division between her breasts. Meredith was very controlled and was as polite to her as to Jane, who wore a beige cashmere dress—very suitable. But I could see him looking at Samantha's dangling earrings, her untidy mass of curly hair, her *chest,* and his eyes were like stones. Gerald looked cross and uncomfortable, although I think they were doing something with their feet under the table. Jane was perfect, of course, and tried to draw Samantha into the conversation; but none of her topics seemed to be in areas that interested Samantha. She mentioned Junior League activities, a recent trip to Europe, inflation, the Princess of Wales's children, a whole spectrum of subjects; but Samantha had almost nothing to say. She is quite pretty, or would be if she would comb her hair and do something about her clothes. I can't for the life of me understand why Gerald doesn't make her change. He calls her Sam, and when he looks at her—I will admit to you now on paper something that I could never tell you face-to-face—I am jealous. No man has ever looked at me that way—as though he were seeing a vision—something delectable, desirable, but sparked with grace. But it is the tenderness that really eats into my heart, and fills me with an envy as green as grass. I said that no one had ever looked at me like that, but that's not strictly true. There was Jamie. I thought about Jamie as I watched them. Then I tried to concentrate on the turkey, on the preparation and serving of food. I couldn't cope with all the conflicting things I was feeling, or with the vibrations shooting back and forth across the table.

January 4

I wrote a lot yesterday, so I needn't write as much today.

My father was the strong parent in our house. My mother was small and mousy, and I can't remember her with anything but gray hair. She wore housedresses out of Eaton's catalog and no makeup. She did everything my father asked or told her to do, and she never argued. I don't ever remember a fight in our house. I was an only child. My father talked a lot. He told us about how to behave, but he was even more eager to discuss sin. He described the wicked people in the congregation and in the town and the evil things they did. It never occurred to me to like these people. Or rarely. Once I started a friendship with a girl called Gertie Bowman and invited her home one day to play. She was a lot of fun, and I loved her laugh, which was a sort of joyful shriek. My father took me aside afterward and told me that her father drank too much, that her mother was a "bad woman," and that it would be a poor example for a minister's daughter to spend much time with people like that. I could see his point. He also talked a great deal about lying and stealing and coveting and cheating. And vanity. One day my mother came home in a cornflower blue dress. She looked pretty, which was unusual for her, and she seemed cheerful and happy. I was so proud of her, and hugged her, and told her how lovely she looked. My father stood up and said, "Where did you get the money?" and she said, "From Aunt Julia, for Christmas." Then he said, "I find the color vulgar, and besides, we could use the money. Even I can tell that that dress was not cheap. We are not royalty. We have no need of such finery." She said, "Yes, Arthur," and left the room. She looked small and tired, even from the back. We never saw the dress again.

I've written more than I intended.

January 5

I wanted so badly to get to heaven when I was small. I still do. It sounded like such a peaceful, shining place. I was scared of God, but I was assured by my father that if I did exactly what He told me to do, He would be kind and loving forever. This meant that I must never, *never* lie or steal or cheat or even think bad thoughts. It was particularly hard not to think bad thoughts, but every time one nudged itself into my head, I would order it out, clench my fists, and try to think of beautiful things. I became very skillful at this, but it took enormous effort.

I always kept hoping that if I did everything right, my father, like God, would also be soft and loving. Sometimes he said, "Good for you, Allison" when I did something *unusually* wonderful, like the time I gave away my new doll to a poor girl on Water Street who had received no Christmas presents. It wasn't my idea, which I suppose would have been better, but at least I did it. But even then he didn't hug me or anything, or say, "I love you," or stroke my hair the way I'd seen other fathers do. Dolls' heads were made of china then, with soft cloth bodies. She had blue eyes, just like real eyes, with eyelashes, and they opened and closed when you changed the position of her head. She had a mauve dress with ruffles on the skirt and a headful of tiny black curls—real hair, not just painted on.

January 6

I'm too tired today to write. Gerald came to see his father this morning, and they were in Meredith's study for twenty-five minutes. Although I couldn't hear what they were saying, I didn't like the sound of their voices. When they came out, Meredith was looking pale and frozen, but saying nothing. Gerald turned to his father and said, "I'm *twenty-six,* Dad!" with a look on his face that I can't even describe. Then he dashed out of the house, slamming the door, without even looking at me. Meredith stood perfectly still in the front hall, and then went back into his study, closing the door with exaggerated care.

I wish I didn't have this awful desire to cry all the time.

January 7

When I saw you today, you said that I must try to write about the past, even if my mind is preoccupied with the present. It's all right, you said, to mention what's going on now, but that I might find everything, including the present, easier to cope with if I dug up all that really old stuff.

I forgot to mention that the day I gave away my doll, my mother cried. I can't remember if I did. I can't remember anything else at all about that day.

January 8

"I will never, never forgive you if I ever catch you lying." That is exactly what my father said to me that day in June. I can hear him still, as clearly as if it were yesterday. He had seen a neighboring boy, Joe Hamandi was his name, steal one of our daffodils the day before. The next day, when Joe appeared on the sidewalk, Father rushed out to scold him, to punish him. His face was red with anger, and his eyes were like black bullets. "How dare you pick one of our flowers!" he shouted, waving his fist. "How dare you steal my property!" The little boy was white with fright. "I didn't! I didn't!" he whispered. "Someone else did it! *I* didn't!" And then he ran away. "Liar! Liar!" yelled my father. "Worse by far than a thief!" And then he told me what he would do to me if he ever caught me lying.

Gerald wants to marry Samantha. We are all in a state of shock. Jane and Luther won't even discuss it with him, and Meredith, of course, is beside himself.

I don't know what to do. Worse still, I don't even know what to think.

January 9

This is a bad part and will be hard for me to tell. But I don't have to show it to you if I don't want to. You told me that.

One day when I was eight years old, Father was in a terrible mood. It was Saturday, which meant that he was writing his sermon, and he was always nervous on those days. I was playing hopscotch on the pattern of the parlor rug, when suddenly I tripped and fell against a table. The table swayed and then righted itself, but not before a glass lamp fell over onto the floor and broke in a thousand pieces. My father heard the crash and came rushing in, pen in one hand, a sheet of paper in the other. He saw the lamp immediately, and fixed me with his terrible look. "Who did that?" he roared. "Did you break that lamp?"

"No!" The answer was out before I had time to think. "The dog rushed by just now and caught the cord! And over it went! Jason! It was Jason!" My fear had been terrible, but what I was feeling now was a hundred times worse. I stood on the carpet as though turned to stone, listening while he shouted for Jason. Then I held my hands over my ears while he beat the dog, hearing his squeals through my palms.

I went into my room and crawled into bed, making myself as small as possible. I cannot describe the weight of my guilt. When Jason crept into the room, tail between his legs, I picked him up and held him with a shame and a remorse that was boundless, patting him, stroking him, whispering, "I'm sorry! I'm sorry! Forgive me, Jason!" I knew I must confess, and yet I also knew I must *not* confess, all at the same time. For if I did tell him, my father would never forgive me that lie; if I did not, I felt that the warm face of heaven would be hidden from me for all time, that God would forever turn His back upon me. I didn't cry. Sorrow was not what I was feeling. I felt a numbing fear and a regret so deep that I was drowning in it. Lost grace. That's what I felt. Grace irrevocably removed from me.

I feel so ashamed of the things I have told you about my father. I have made him sound like an ogre in a fairy tale. He wasn't. He gave away a fifth of his small salary to the church. He allowed himself no luxuries. He visited the sick and the dying, and his sermons were thrilling, inspiring. Ladies in the congregation sometimes cried while he was speaking. He wanted everyone in the world to be good.

You maybe can't believe it, but I worried about that lamp, that lie, for four years. I rehearsed speeches that I never delivered; I prayed for forgiveness, but felt there could be no forgiveness without confession. I would watch other children playing, strangers walking briskly along the street, animals running in the fields and think, "Oh, to be one of them, without this binding burden on my heart." I went about my everyday living—going to school, playing ball, drying the dishes—but always in a small part of my heart or head was this hard core of guilt, this feeling that I was doomed unless or until I told my father what had really happened to that lamp.

Samantha came and talked to me today. I like her. She lacks refinement, but she is warm and quick and passionate, which is more than you can say of either Luther or his father—both cold fish, and very virtuous and upright. And controlled. It is a terrible and unnatural thing to say about one's own son, but I do not altogether like Luther. I love him, of course. That is a different thing entirely. But his heart is squeezed and arrogant, and I often do not like him at all. Gerald is the spontaneous one, and kind.

As for me, I don't know what I am.

But I can tell you one thing. I can feel it in the air. Samantha likes me.

January 11

I know I'll never be able to show you this book. I reread yesterday's entry and was shocked to see that I had called my own son and my husband *cold fish.*

I broke the lamp when I was eight. One day when I was twelve, my father and I were looking through an old family album in the parlor. "Wait," he said. "It's getting dark. I'll get a lamp." He brought a lamp from his study and placed it on the same table that had held the first ill-fated lamp. I heard myself speaking as though it were someone else, as though a piece of quite casual information were being offered. I had rehearsed the words so often that when they finally came out they emerged without tone or emphasis. They might have been the tapping of typewriter keys.

"Father," I heard the voice say. "Remember the old glass lamp? The one that used to be on this table?"

"Uh? Oh, yes, I guess so."

"Well, it was me that broke it."

I don't know what I expected. Probably a spectacular display of rage or an icy comment upon my sin, followed by a promise of eternal damnation. I think I had also half hoped for a thunder of drums or the sweet swell of violin strings, to accompany the end of my long period of fear and guilt.

But not much of anything happened.

"Oh?" he said. "Did you?" But I could see that he had long ago forgotten the episode. Or possibly he was too preoccupied by what he was looking at to pay much attention. Not that it mattered all that much, not really. It is true that I was relieved. But I also knew in that moment, without the smallest doubt, that crime never pays. If retribution does not come from without, it will surely always come from within. Look at what I had suffered during the past four years. I would watch my step even more carefully in future.

January 12

I can see by looking at old photographs that as a teenager I was pretty. I was also shapely. I can remember Mother's shy remarks to me about my clothes. "Your father wants you to stop wearing that red dress, dear. He says that it makes your bust too obvious. He says that modesty is a woman's most attractive feature." I think now that she said this a bit wistfully, being flat as a board herself. I would have felt better if he had called breasts *breasts*. Bust is a terrible word. It smacks of corseted spinsters or of plaster of Paris. When I wore the clothes I liked, I felt cheap and vulgar. When I wore the kind of things he wanted me to wear, I felt droopy, desexed, undesirable. Either way I was a loser.

But Jamie desired me. Blousy tops, loose waists and all, he still looked at me as though I were a mixture of Lana Turner, a chocolate milkshake, and a delicate flower.

January 13

I am going to write about Jamie now.

Jamie worked at Sullivan's Garage after school, so he didn't have much time for parties or dating. But during the spring when I was sixteen, he spent every one of his spare moments stationed in the vacant lot across the road from our house, or walking up and down the street, kicking stones in front of him as he went. If I came out the front door, his face would burst wide open with joy, and he would come forward to accompany me wherever I was going. When Father found out that his mother had once been charged with petty theft, he told me that I must never bring him into the house and that I must never under any circumstances accept any invitations from him. But even Father could not refuse him access to the vacant lot or to the municipal sidewalk. Or so I thought.

One day, quite by accident, I saw Jamie downtown. We met eye to eye over the mittens and gloves section of Woolworth's; face aflame, he reached over and touched one of my cheeks and then kissed me most tenderly on the other. Such an innocent and lovely thing. It was my first kiss of any kind, and I came very close indeed to falling headfirst into the mittens. But Father saw us; he was standing not ten feet away, in the hardware department.

When I returned home, Father explained to me where such behavior might lead. To the Devil, to Hell, to social disgrace, but more important, to the East Concook Home for unmarried mothers. One day when I returned alone from an errand downtown, I saw Father talking to Jamie at the end of our walk. They were both gone by the time I reached the house, so I never knew what had taken place between them. But Jamie never returned. The vacant lot remained vacant, and the sidewalk bare. I thought I would die, but I did not.

January 14

I have just reread what I wrote yesterday, and it all came back to me so vividly. Not my love for Jamie, but the sweet heat and flavor of that time.

I don't think I feel like writing today.

January 16

After Jamie, Father was vigilant. I was young, too young to marry. But if there had been one Jamie, there might be others. Father really did love me. He wanted me to be safe. Safe for what? For heaven, I guess. Or for my own life, although that's hardly likely. Maybe for *him,* for his love and anxiety's sake. I must try to believe that, because I'm crying less these past few days. Instead, I'm feeling angry.

Father brought Meredith home for dinner because he was new in town and probably lonely. Or so he said. More than likely, for a certainty, in fact, he had checked his credentials. Twenty-eight to my eighteen. Staunch member of the Presbyterian church and a generous contributor to the building fund. Immaculately dressed in navy suits with white shirts, blindingly white, with starched collars. Well spoken. Courteous. Six feet one inch, undeniably handsome. And with a good, dependable job.

Gerald came to me today and begged me to argue his case with his father. He is very unhappy. I went to Meredith and told him I thought Samantha was a kind and loving person, and that Gerald was after all an adult who should make his own decisions. You cannot imagine how much courage it took for me to do this. Or maybe you can, it being your business to understand this kind of thing. Meredith does not rant and rave like Father. This quality is what drew me to him in the first place. I did not then realize that anger has many faces, and that there are a lot of subtler forms of violence and violation. Meredith looked at me very coldly and said, "I cannot imagine how anyone supposedly clever can be so stupid. You claim to love this boy, and yet you are perfectly willing to wreck his life. I forbid you to side with him. Your view of love is naive and permissive. Kindly leave this matter entirely to me." When I tried to interrupt, he broke in and said, "Allison. If you please. I do not wish to discuss this further."

I can't really see that writing all these things down is very helpful. It is true that I am crying less. But I'm not sure that it is any improvement to be feeling this terrible new anger and frustration.

I gathered up some rugs today and hung them outside on the line. Then I took a heavy stick and beat them and beat them, until the yard was a fog of dust. I did not even feel tired when I finished, and then I went inside and slept for two hours. Meredith was not pleased when supper was late, but said nothing. He sighed a great deal, however. I wanted to kick him. Or to hang him on the line and beat him with a stick.

January 20

I'm remembering things that I must have shoved away to the back of my mind. I don't understand how your brain can let this happen. Surely significant things, good or bad, should be written in headlines on the forefront of one's brain. But no. Apparently not.

I have remembered something that happened the summer after my innocent fling with Jamie. I was seventeen, and I was delivering some of my mother's homemade bread to an old lady who was sick. Mrs. Bellamy was her name. She lived on the other side of town, and I took a shortcut across O'Malley's field to get there. This was not really a field, but a wild rough place with two hills, a lot of bushes, and a little creek. On my way across the smaller of the hills, I decided to go down by the creek to see if there were any Indian pipes. What I found by the edge of the water were not Indian pipes, but my father and Miss Henderson, the director of the junior choir. They were kissing. They didn't see me.

Try as I will, I can't remember one single other thing about that morning. Whether or not the bread ever reached old Mrs. Bellamy I do not know. However, I do recall hearing my mother and father talking in the kitchen that afternoon. She was speaking.

"Mr. O'Toole said he tried to get you on the church phone this morning, but that no one answered."

There was a pause. And then my father said, "Then he must have been calling the wrong number. I never left the office all morning."

I now recollect trying to argue myself out of what I

had seen and heard, much as one tries to talk oneself into a belief in Santa Claus after seeing one's mother filling the stockings. Maybe that wasn't really my father down there. I brushed aside the evidence—his diamond socks (knitted by my mother) sticking out below his trouser cuffs; his briefcase on the ground beside him, with his gold initials on it (gift of the Missionary Society)—and said to myself, *It was not him, it was not him.* And if it had not been my father, then I had not heard him tell that lie. Then I forgot about it for thirty-eight years.

Meredith has told Gerald that if he marries Samantha he must leave the company, Meredith Wentworth and Sons Limited. Gerald came and asked my opinion and advice. He said he had always hated working for the company anyway, but had done it because of "family pressure." Family pressure, my foot, I thought. Let us call a spade a spade, if you please. Father pressure. I knew that Gerald had once wanted to be a garage mechanic; as Jamie had been exactly that, I guess I had not looked on it as such a disgraceful thing to be. But Meredith had refused to consider it for two seconds. Pride. The First Deadly Sin.

I told Gerald that I had been forbidden to offer advice or to discuss this matter with him.

"Please, Mom," he begged. "*Please.* I probably know

what I'm going to do anyway, but tell me what you think, how you feel about it."

"Do you love her a great deal?" I asked.

"Yes," he said. "Oh yes."

"Then leave," I said. "The company will survive. And so will we. And so will you." Then I kissed him.

I am feeling neither angry nor weepy tonight. I am feeling rather pleased with myself.

February 1

What a month this has been. I may become a chronic diarist. I won't pretend that it solves everything. I'm feeling like a cracked egg—very, very fragile. But *ready*. Do you know what I mean?

When Meredith heard from Gerald that he was leaving the company, he came to me and cried. *Cried!* If you had asked me, I would have said that all Meredith's tears had dried up at birth, that there was no room in this man for fury or grief or for passionate responses. So life is full of surprises. I comforted him. I felt like the strong one.

And that night I was visited by another memory.

When I was eighteen years old—several months before I met Meredith—I was struck by a car. I was not hurt, but I was taken to the hospital for a routine examination. Insurance regulations required it. Word reached my parents that there had been an accident, before they received the news that I had not been injured. When they arrived at the hospital, Father pushed my mother aside and rushed to where I sat on a straight chair in the emergency ward. He took me in his arms and held me so tightly that I remember hurting all over. "Thank God, thank God you're safe!" he gasped. "Oh, Allison, I'm so sorry, so sorry! Forgive me. Try to forgive me. Oh, my child, thank God you are safe!" Then he put his head down on my shoulder and cried like a child. Much of that scene is fuzzy in my memory. And I don't know what any of it means, or why I forgot it. But whatever else he may have meant, I can see now that two messages were clear. One, he was a human being after all. Two, he loved me very much. In any case, my moment of truth was short-lived, because I fainted soon afterward. When I came to, the scene was locked away where it was very hard to find.

February 15

Samantha and Gerald are to be married on April 2nd. Meredith has told Gerald that he may remain in the company after all, but Gerald has informed him (very nicely) that (thank you very much) he's already been accepted for a course in auto mechanics at the community college.

He has some money saved. Besides, Samantha has a job. Meredith took this hard, but he is trying to adjust to all the new things that are happening to him. Luther is not trying to adjust to anything at all, although yesterday I astonished him by telling him he was an insufferable snob. I hope he will think about that. If this makes him angry with me, that's just too bad. Jane can prop him up, and I'm sure she will.

Samantha's mother died when she was ten, so I am helping her with her wedding dress. She has a flair for design, and I am good with a needle. The pattern is a bit extreme, but she has the looks and the figure to carry it off. We will keep it our secret until the wedding day. She is warm and communicative, and I think she is going to be the daughter I have always longed for. She says she has a lot to learn from me. She doesn't realize how much I need to learn from her.

Meredith will be all right. He hasn't really changed. It's just that now I'm ready to see things in him that must have been there all along. If you lie right down on your belly, yes, I said *belly,* with your face pressed flat into the floor, you can't criticize people if they walk over you. My mother was a doormat all her life, and I can't say I look back on her with any feeling stronger than a tender pity. I know it irritated Meredith when I was going through that weepy phase, and I can't say I blame him. Yesterday he said something arrogant to me, and I said to him, "Meredith, you are not God Almighty, and I would appreciate a little humility around here." He was obviously dumbfounded; but it was also clear that he preferred this approach to that of the teary-eyed wimp. He is not my idea of Lochinvar riding out of the west, and never was. But we'll manage. We'll be fine.

I never had any intention of showing you this diary. Not really. But maybe I will. I'm even tempted to invite you to the wedding. I feel that you are sort of responsible for it. One way or another.

The Courtship

Mr. VANBUSKIRK SAT on his veranda, rocking. He lifted his eyes—heavy-lidded and remarkably sexy for a man of eighty years—and looked upon the day. "A day like any other day," he mused aloud. But he was wrong. It was not.

Down the street, Mrs. Knickle, who slept better than Mr. VanBuskirk, opened her eyes and observed the bright June morning, watching the mottled light dance upon her ceiling. Reaching out to a glass on her night table, she dipped slender, skillful fingers into the water and fished out her teeth. Popping them into her mouth with a delicate expertise, she smiled quietly, her face transformed. Next, she cupped her hands and placed all eight fingers and both thumbs under her hairnet, lifting it carefully from a profuse but untangled mass of chalk white curls. No blue rinse here, but a very expensive wash-and-wear perm from Les Cheveux, last Thursday. She patted her curls gently and could feel that the spring had survived the night. Putting on a pair of rimless glasses, adjusting the curved metal sides around her ears, she checked her watch. Eight o'clock. She counted on her fingers, moving her lips. Nine hours. Subtract the hour in the middle of the night, which had followed a trip to the bathroom. Eight hours. Very good. She smiled again, somewhat smugly. No one else in her peer group could boast of eight hours' sleep every night. Over coffee, they spoke of insomnia, the late show, night prowling, and discussed "dwindling need." Nonsense, thought Mrs. Knickle. She needed that eight hours. In fact, she felt that very few of her needs had dwindled.

Reaching down under the covers, Mrs. Knickle smoothed her blue nylon nightgown (gift from Mary on Mother's Day of a year ago) over her spare body. As her hands passed over her thighs, she frowned slightly. *Lank shanks.* Somebody had said that, some writer, a poet maybe; her memory had become so unpredictable of late. The phrase hung in the air. She felt it had something to do with age, and she knew it was not a compliment. Mrs. Knickle was seventy-seven years old.

As was her wont when faced with an unpleasant fact,

Mrs. Knickle looked at it as briefly as possible and then averted her gaze, switching her channel to a better picture. She tested her resting heart rate, pressing the carotid artery in her neck and counting the seconds on her wristwatch. She tipped her head in order to accommodate her bifocals. Sixty-two. Very good, indeed. Her brisk, daily two-mile walk was paying off. Mrs. Knickle stretched and flexed the muscles of her thin arms and legs. Almost no arthritis, despite that week-long period of damp Nova Scotia weather. She continued to smile at the shivering dappled ceiling. She was ready. For the day, and for whatever else might present itself.

Slithering out of bed with catlike agility, Mrs. Knickle stood erect, pulling her five-feet-one-inch form up to its full height. She padded quickly out to the kitchen on bare feet and made herself a cup of tea. Bringing it back to the bedroom, she placed it on the night table and plumped up three fat pillows. Then she climbed back into bed. Looking out the east window at the sparkling new day and drinking her tea, she decided to plan strategy. Mrs. Knickle had not lost the habit of hope. Cheerfully and tenaciously, she clung to the custom of expectation. For example, she *expected* each morning to receive a letter in the mail. She applied this outlook to almost all of her life. She was about to do this now.

One of the pleasures of living alone, she thought, as she took another sip of tea—postponing strategy for a moment—was that you could do, in private, all the things frowned on by society. As, for instance, with the slurping of one's tea. She slurped contentedly. Belching was also permitted in a world that contained no one to hear it. And other censored things. She chuckled into her tea. Basil had been against just about everything. Against noise (gastronomical, musical, social, conversational, and the kinds made by children), Irish Catholics, and social-ism. Also underdone meat, laziness, and Mrs. Knickle's predilection for the color purple. She had loved him and mourned him; but she remembered the morning when she first emerged from her loneliness and grief to sniff the heady scent of freedom.

It had been, of all things, a bleak November day, with the rain pouring down in wind-driven sheets from the southeast. She had looked out at it and addressed her canary. "When I was a child, I loved just such a day." Then she had suddenly stood up a little straighter and looked about her with a kind of wonder. A soft, surprised warmth spread through her chest cavity. There was no one there to speak of sloth, no one to make disparaging remarks about her choice of reading materials. She could do it. She could read all day if she wished. Plato's *Republic* or a trashy novel. Take your pick. Quickly she had laid and lit a fire in the living room, brewed enough coffee to last the day, crawled back into her housecoat, and read for six hours. At noon she had taken a small glass of sherry, sipping it slowly. Then she had planned the rest of her life, as she looked out the window at the driving rain. "We could need another ark before this storm is over," she had said aloud, "and if there is one, I mean to be on it."

That was ten years ago. She had been sixty-seven then, and young. Seventy-seven was not old, she mused, but it was undeniably moving in that direction. Ten years, she felt, is long enough to be free. She had been sensing a niggling urge, of late, for companionship—companionship of the kind that only a husband could give. She wanted someone who was always *there,* not someone you called and arranged to meet for lunch or a person you dropped in on for coffee. She was starting to crave a live-in presence to whom she would be Number One. Who would listen to her theories about life or to her informative and unmalicious gossip about the citizens of the town. Who would cherish her diffuse general chitter-chatter.

A good cook, she longed for someone with whom

she could share her excellent meals. Basil had always relished her cooking and had told her so. He had been as opposed to ingratitude as he had been to noise and purple and Catholics. He had also been against dishonesty and cruelty and the depredation of the forests. It is true that he had sometimes been dishonest with *himself,* and could be cruel without even knowing he was doing it. And consistency had not been his strong point. It was during his presidency of the local Committee for the Reforestation of Our Country that he had cut down her favorite dogwood tree without even consulting her. He was a horticultural snob and felt that dogwood was a lower-class tree. Furthermore, he had just simply assumed that she would agree with his point of view. Her frequent comments over the years on the dogwood's beauty (blossoms, leaves, berries) had apparently slid past his ears, unperceived.

Basil had been opinionated and domineering, but Mrs. Knickle had to concede that he had grown up in an environment that fostered this kind of nonsense in men. And it was one of the sad facts of present-day feminism, she felt, that it had created, fully armed, as it were, a host of opinionated and domineering women out of what had been a lot of rather nice people. The old order had been bad, certainly, but what it had yielded to was sometimes not much better. Some women, she had observed, solved their problems by simply placing themselves on the other side of the seesaw. She was ready to move back to an area of middle ground.

She had intended to plan strategy, but she found herself continuing to think about Basil. If one chose, one could shove most of the blame onto Basil's mother for bringing him up to be so pushy. But in the long haul, it had been she, Mrs. Knickle, who had let the results of his mother's training prevail. She could, she knew, have stood up for Catholics, eaten rare beef, and worn purple. But she had simply switched her emotional channel on and off for thirty-five years. She had walked around Basil's offending attitudes when she should have been kicking them into the corner. But the time for fretting about this was long past.

She enjoyed good memories of Basil. He had adored her in his own way, had found her beautiful. Shortsighted in so many other areas, he had also failed to see that she was too short, too thin—indeed virtually without any shape at all—and that her features (described by some as birdlike) were uncompromisingly sharp. He had been good in bed; and at times of extreme pain (when Mary had rheumatic fever, when Chuck had that awful car accident in high school, each time one of her canaries died), his comfort had been sustaining and generous. All things considered, and given the temper of the times, Mrs. Knickle felt that it had been a good marriage.

And now she had had her fill of independence, of widowhood. It was 1984. Time was passing. She wanted someone else in that house with her. She wanted a person to snuggle up to in bed, to enjoy her coq au vin, to ask about her day. She also suspected that she was at least slightly in love.

Four houses away, Mr. VanBuskirk rocked back and forth on his veranda. Between his own spruce tree and the house across the street, he could see the harbor glistening in the early morning sun. A good town to live in, he reflected. Never more than a quarter mile from the sea. Or a lake, or some kind of water. "I could not survive without water," he said aloud.

"No one can," said a cheeky voice from the sidewalk. Ogden Johnston faced him from the bottom of the veranda's wooden steps. "The teacher says no one can. Not even people who are *young*. So it must be extra important for *you*." Ogden was eight years old.

Mr. VanBuskirk looked at Ogden's bland face. "I wasn't talking about that kind of water," he said coldly. "I was referring to something more spiritual. Something more aesthetic."

"My brother has asthma, too," Ogden said. "But he doesn't talk to himself. You do."

Mr. VanBuskirk chose not to reply.

"My mother says it's a real bad sign to talk to yourself," Ogden continued.

"I almost never talk to myself."

Ogden had been raised to believe that it was a virtue to express himself. His mother was a painter, and his father wrote bad poetry. "You do so. I hear you. Often. Behind the screen door. Talking and talking."

"Probably on the telephone or calling the cat. And why?"

"Why what?"

"Why is it a bad sign?"

"I don't know. I'll ask my mom. Then I'll let you know." Swinging his antique yo-yo, taking care not to step on any sidewalk cracks, Ogden walked crookedly down the block to his house. He lived next door to Mrs. Knickle.

Mrs. Knickle saw Ogden enter his house, banging the screen door behind him. She wondered, as she had done for over fifty years, why children found it necessary to slam doors, while most adults simply shut them. It was one of the few things in life that irritated her. She frowned and made a mental list: slamming doors;

chewing food with one's mouth open; drying dishes too slowly; removing nail polish with one's teeth, with accompanying scraping noises; all forms of nose picking. And dogs that yap.

Clucking at her current canary on her way to the kitchen, Mrs. Knickle made her breakfast and prepared herself for the day. For one whole hour she had let her mind wander from the matter at hand. Strategy.

She was too old for the hard-to-get approach. That procedure called for youth, when you had all the time in the world in which to lay the groundwork. Of course, subtlety would be required, just as it was in all exchanges between people. The direct slam-bang system almost never worked, and she had always been far too pragmatic to use methods that were not practical. No. She would assess Mr. VanBuskirk as best she could, and then work out a way—slithering sideways—to walk straight into his heart.

Mrs. Knickle's knowledge of Mr. VanBuskirk was sparse. He had moved into his house on Spruce Street five years after Basil died. He was a retired university professor—of what, she did not know—and she assumed that his mind must therefore be full of profundities and intricate sensitivities. This appealed to her. Basil had been a dedicated laboratory technician whose conversation had not been stimulating. Her family had felt that she had married below her intellectual level; but he had had marvelous cheekbones and massive shoulders, and she had not listened to their counsel.

Mrs. Knickle's contacts with Mr. VanBuskirk had consisted of "hellos" and "good mornings" as one or the other of them had passed by. Or when they met on the bus. She had always enjoyed observing his long, lank frame (in a different category entirely from lank shanks) as well as his bedroom eyes—enormous, brown, with what she felt was a lingering regard. Shaded lids. Hiding complicated thoughts; telling nothing. Eyes to be reckoned with.

Then Mrs. Knickle had attended a community meeting to protest the building of a high-rise factory structure directly beside the town's public park. Mr. VanBuskirk had arrived, clothed in a highly becoming Stewart plaid shirt; he also had worn a pair of jeans that had shown off his flat stomach. She had looked around at the paunches with which she was surrounded. Ogden's father, only thirty-five years old, had a stomach that lopped over his belt, almost obscuring it. Their town councillor, Mr. Wesley Rankin, sported chins as well as stomachs. The men must have outweighed the women, four to one.

At the meeting, Mr. VanBuskirk had sat down, hands

placed on his knees, perfectly still, speaking to no one. Mysterious, thought Mrs. Knickle. Enigmatic. He doesn't look unfriendly. He just looks . . . contained. Then, when Mr. Gilbert Hogan rose to discuss progress and business acumen in connection with the new factory, Mr. VanBuskirk got up slowly from his chair; he stood tall, still, dignified—no fidgeting, no tics—and addressed the gathering. Mrs. Knickle envisioned him in a toga. She fitted him with a laurel wreath and then discarded it. The plaid shirt kept intruding, and his hair was wrong.

But his speech. Oh, how she loved his speech. Talking slowly, but with emphasis and considerable rhetorical flair, he used his magnificent bass voice to good effect.

"I did not return to Nova Scotia from the arid wastes of Ontario in order to watch the march of progress," he began. "There is quite enough of that to be found west of the Isthmus of Chignecto, creating, I might say, pollution, economic imbalance, labor unrest, and foul working conditions—not to mention a wealth of human greed." He paused and gazed around the audience, eyes steady.

"No!" His voice rose, and the audience started. "I returned to Nova Scotia to reclaim the values that enriched my childhood in this small town. I came back to nourish my old age in an atmosphere of wise and balanced thinking. I settled here in order to find tranquility beside an unravaged sea, to see again the land where beauty and equilibrium prevail."

Mrs. Knickle felt an odd sensation move up and down her spinal column.

Mr. VanBuskirk fixed Mr. Gilbert Hogan with unwavering eyes. "I did not come here in order to see a beautiful park overshadowed by a hideous concrete structure, casting shade on the flowers, discouraging the visitation of wild fowl, filling the air with honking cars, screaming brakes, choking smoke. No! I returned to my native province because I knew—where my confidence was strong—that enlightened attitudes would inhabit the minds of my neighbors. Where I felt that no one would value a dollar more than a flower. Where loveliness and nature would always outweigh the temptations of so-called progress and prosperity."

Someone in the back row yelled out something about jobs and hunger, but he was loudly shushed by the chairman of the meeting. The vote for the factory lost by an enormous margin. Although many people pressed forward to thank Mr. VanBuskirk, he was nowhere to be found. He had chosen a seat near the door and had slipped out. Mrs. Knickle went home and slept unusually

lightly, visited by dreams whose contents were surprising
in a woman of seventy-seven years.

Mrs. Knickle now set down her dishcloth and took
out a pad. On it she wrote:

> *Description:*
> (Assets)
> Intelligent
> Educated
> Confident
> Thin
> Loves beauty
> Hates pollution
> Very sexy
> Not chatty
> Has pension (presumably)
> Very desirable
> Excellent values
> Subtle charisma

It was a daunting list, but Mrs. Knickle was not easily
cowed. On the opposite page she wrote:

> *Strategy:*
> Lead from strength.

Which was? Find common areas and start there. She cast her eye over the list and decided that she more or less shared all the qualities, with the possible exception of "very sexy" and "not chatty" and "subtle charisma." But opposites often attract. Basil had been tall and exceedingly handsome. Ready to leap into bed at a moment's notice, he had, after all, chosen to leap with her.

"We live ever in hope," said Mrs. Knickle.

A face appeared at the screen door.

"You, too?" it said, and then Ogden walked in, bearing a measuring cup. "My mom says can we borrow a cup of white sugar?"

"Me, too, what?" Mrs. Knickle asked, and then, "No, you can't. I only have brown. White is unhealthy."

"Talk to yourself," Ogden said. "Okay, I'll try Mr. VanBuskirk. I got something to tell him anyways." And he was gone, slamming the door behind him.

On his veranda, Mr. VanBuskirk watched the approach of Ogden and meditated on the youth of today. Fancy a child of 1910 daring to suggest to one's betters and one's elders that they talked to themselves. Nevertheless, it was interesting. He wondered if Ogden had consulted his scatterbrained mother—the one who painted those unbridled abstract flower pictures—as to the dangers of talking to oneself. He chuckled deep in his throat and then changed, when Ogden started to climb the steps, to what he hoped was a stern harrumph.

"I need some white sugar for Mom's trifle," Ogden announced, holding out his measuring cup on a straight arm. "It's made of cake and jam and custard. And white sugar. Mrs. Knickle only has brown."

"Very well," Mr. VanBuskirk said, without moving. "However, first I'd like to know if you have approached your good mother on the subject of speaking to oneself."

"Yes," said Ogden. "I have."

"Well?"

"Crazy or old. Sometimes both."

"So! That's the way it is. Old, I can accept. Crazy pleases me less. But one must bow to what the gods decree. Sugar, you say?"

"Yes. White. One cup."

Mr. VanBuskirk rose slowly and took the measuring cup. He entered the house, slamming the screen door behind him. "Crazy and old, eh?" he muttered. Returning with the sugar, he continued, "Damn sight more interesting to converse with myself than with most other people in this two-bit town." He opened the screen door onto the veranda. "Here," he said to Ogden. "Take your youth and your sanity and your sugar back to your own house."

Ogden grabbed the sugar. "Thanks," he yelled over his shoulder as he leapt down the stairs two at a time, spilling sugar on every step.

Mr. VanBuskirk settled back to his chair and his book, admitting to himself that a little of the glitter had gone out of the day.

Four houses down the street, Mrs. Knickle watched the return of Ogden.

"Get your sugar?" she called down from her veranda.

"Yeah. Old guy talks to himself a lot." He looked at her, sugar trailing out of the tipping cup. "Guess you all do."

Mrs. Knickle frowned. "What I don't understand is who first decided that self-expression was more valuable than manners."

"What? Whatcha say?"

"Nothing. Nothing important. I was just talking to myself."

"My mom says that's a bad sign."

"That's just fine. She is certainly welcome to any diagnosis she may care to make. But I, for one, am not interested in the details. Not in the slightest. Good morning, Ogden."

Ogden went.

"Well," Mrs. Knickle said as she entered the house,

closing the door quietly behind her. "Ogden may not be my favorite person, but he has provided me with a significant maneuver in my campaign. One must give the devil his due, even when he arrives in Levi's."

The morning was a delightful one—sunny and warm for June, with an invigorating breeze that held a mixture of salt and fish and late lilac. Down by the waterfront could be heard the distant thunk of fish boxes and the intermittent call of male voices. Young Mrs. Ernst was wheeling her newest baby down the sidewalk to the accompanying music of the carriage's squeaky wheels. Her three older children trailed behind her, a small parade.

Mrs. Knickle was preparing for her two-mile walk. But today, instead of walking toward the park, she would direct her route past Mr. VanBuskirk's veranda.

Dressed in a pair of gray corduroy pants, a purple sweater, and Birkenstock sandals, Mrs. Knickle set off. Nearing Mr. VanBuskirk's veranda, she slowed. Good. He was there, on his usual chair, reading.

Resolutely, Mrs. Knickle stopped at the foot of his steps and said, "Good morning, Professor VanBuskirk."

Mr. VanBuskirk raised his head, startled. He took off his glasses and rose from his chair.

"Good morning, Miss . . . ," he began uncertainly. Third interruption today, he noted darkly.

"Mrs. Knickle," she announced. "Grace Knickle.

Forgive me for interrupting you in the middle of your studies, but I just wanted to congratulate you."

Mr. VanBuskirk rallied. It had been quite some time since anyone had congratulated him on anything at all. He had long professed that praise was an unnecessary frill. In fact, he had never been able to understand the late Mrs. VanBuskirk's desire for it. "How do I look?" she would ask anxiously, before they left for a faculty reception. Irritated, he had tended to answer, "Fine. Fine. You always look fine. I would let you know if you didn't." Or she would say, "How was the dinner? Did you like the new recipe?" He had eaten it, hadn't he? Why did Myra need to be forever and ever reinforced? In those days he had felt himself to be impervious to both praise and negative criticism. When his lectures were successful (and they usually were) and the students said so (as they often did), well and good. If the group found him to be dull, to hell with them. It was their loss. The lectures were always full of useful facts. A lecture shouldn't have to be a vaudeville act. If he had wanted to entertain, he could have trained as a comedian.

Mr. VanBuskirk looked at Mrs. Knickle with new interest. Ogden had delivered insanity and senility to him earlier this morning. A compliment—or, as she was saying, congratulations—would be a welcome contrast.

"Whatever for?" he asked, and then, "Won't you sit

179

down?" He pulled up a chair from a corner of the veranda and brushed it off with his pocket handkerchief. Mrs. Knickle mounted the steps and sat.

"On your excellent presentation to the town meeting last month. On your content. And, for that matter. . ."—she gazed demurely at her hands in her lap—". . . your delivery. I was very moved."

Mrs. Knickle was surprised by her forwardness. Young girls brought up in the second decade of the twentieth century were taught never to be socially aggressive, especially with gentlemen. And this kind of training dies hard. But she lacked the time for outdated formalities.

"Why, thank you, Mrs. Knickle," Mr. VanBuskirk said, his face serious, his amazing eyes inscrutable.

"The main reason I'm here, however," she went on, "is to say that I'm sorry to have foisted Ogden upon you this morning."

"You foisted Ogden upon me?"

Mrs. Knickle proffered a small smile. "Well, in a manner of speaking. He came to me for white sugar. And I had only brown. It's supposed to be healthier, and at my age, I need all the help I can get." She laughed lightly.

Mr. VanBuskirk looked at Mrs. Knickle's cheerful

face and sprightly movements and felt depressingly old. She must be many years younger than he was. Sixty-six? At most, a youthful sixty-nine.

"Well," he said, suddenly resolving to be honest. "According to Ogden, I need an enormous amount of help. He caught me conversing with the ether. Told me that talking to myself was an ominous sign. I was unwise enough to ask him to elucidate."

"And?"

"It seems I am either crazy or old. Or both."

"If so," announced Mrs. Knickle jubilantly, "then there are two crazy people on the block."

And presumably old, too. Mr. VanBuskirk's spirits rose.

"I've been talking to myself," she continued, "ever since I learned to speak, at eleven months."

Mr. VanBuskirk sighed. Oh, well. Bright, apparently. But young. All that energy.

"Now then," Mrs. Knickle said, "I must be off for my daily walk. Oh . . . How did you enjoy the Liberal convention last night? It seemed to me that the wrong man won, and for all the wrong reasons." She waited expectantly, standing.

"I'm a Conservative, myself," he said. "Couldn't care less who wins in that godforsaken party. Who did?"

Mrs. Knickle was thunderstruck and didn't answer. Clearly, political science was not his field. But one expects a certain awareness, a certain concern about matters national and political, no matter what the academic discipline.

"Would you enjoy a lemonade?" Mr. VanBuskirk asked suddenly. "It could help you on your walk. Give you strength, perhaps."

Mrs. Knickle sat down again. "That would be simply lovely," she said, and looked quietly out at the street as he rose from his seat. Mrs. Ernst was still trailing up and down, up and down the street with her brood; the lilac bush on Mr. VanBuskirk's lawn was at its prime; a butterfly went loping by in the warm air.

Bang! Mr. VanBuskirk slammed the screen door even harder than Ogden as he entered the house. Mrs. Knickle winced, but did so philosophically. One must not expect perfection.

After what seemed to Mrs. Knickle a very long time, Mr. VanBuskirk returned, bearing a tray with two glasses, two napkins, and a plate of dry crackers.

"Sorry," he said. "No cookies or cake. Ogden said his mother needed the sugar for a trifle. I almost said, 'I'll give you a cup of sugar only on the condition that you bring me a dish of trifle for my supper.' But instead, I listened to his insults and let him go, unchallenged. Haven't seen a homemade cookie since Myra died twelve years ago." He wondered vaguely if he was hinting, and hoped not.

Mrs. Knickle was just tucking this bit of information into her mental pocket when a swallow flew into the veranda and lit on a shelf under the eaves.

"Shoo! Shoo!" Mr. VanBuskirk was suddenly awkwardly active, clapping his hands, stomping around the veranda. "That confounded bird has been dickering for a roost on that shelf all week. With any encouragement she'll make a nest and have a whole flock of open-mouthed babies. Then try to read your book in peace. Fat chance. Can't stand birds. Goddamn fluttery things."

A deep sadness settled on Mrs. Knickle's heart. A Conservative, and an ignorant Conservative at that. A door slammer. A hater of birds, and apparently of young things in general. What on earth kind of professor had he been, anyway?

Mrs. Knickle sipped her lemonade. "May I ask you what subject you taught before you retired, Professor VanBuskirk?" She wondered if he didn't like people interrupting his reading, either. But she was really thinking about Christmas and about Mary's children running around making a noise. She could visualize Mr.

VanBuskirk retiring to his study (created from the old playroom in the basement), scowling. She had been going to suggest that he might like to accompany her on her walk. But after watching his slow progress from his rocker to the door and from the door to her chair, she changed her mind. Too slow. He'd never be able to match her pace. Probably be a slow dish dryer, too—if he ever deigned to dry dishes at all.

"Physics," he replied. "The book I'm reading right now is on the quantum theory. Old, but forever new. Was, is, and always will be. The book's a bit old hat, but still intriguing."

"My majors in university were history and English," Mrs. Knickle ventured. "I felt that in studying those two subjects I could come closest to understanding life. One discipline tells it as it really was, the other as the imagination perceives it—which can be even more valid." She had rehearsed this speech this morning, before leaving the house.

"Physics is my life," he continued, starting his sentence before she had quite finished hers. "To me, it is my contact with Cosmos; it is my private denial of Chaos. Mathematics is the great ordering force. Just think! The entire universe, galaxy upon galaxy, moves in accordance with its laws!" His eyes were alive now, sparked by some source of energy that Mrs. Knickle would never understand.

"Myself," she pressed on, "I feel that people are the key to the part of the universe that matters. Simple everyday experiences, culminating in pain or love. These are the things that are of concern to me." Galaxies be darned, she thought.

He did not answer. His gaze was on the lilac bush, but his thoughts were elsewhere. Embracing the quantum theory, she supposed.

Abruptly she got up to leave. "Thank you so much, Professor VanBuskirk, for the lemonade and cracker. Fuel for my walk. And don't worry about talking to yourself. I've been doing it for seventy-five and one-half years."

And started at eleven months. It did not take Mr. VanBuskirk long to do this piece of arithmetic. She was seventy-seven years old. Stunned, he did not even say good-bye. He just raised his hand in a gesture of farewell.

Mrs. Knickle's walk was not a success. She felt tired and moved more slowly than usual. She developed a blister on her right heel and had to stop at Lawton's Drugstore for Band-Aids, lest the blister burst and stain her expensive sandals. She met Ogden later on and he asked, "What's the matter?" What did he mean, *"What's the matter?"* A person must look pretty terrible before someone, even Ogden, asks, "What's the matter?" Ogden was standing beside the town duck pond at the time. She thought about how pleasurable it would be to push him right into the water, to watch him glurp and splutter. She pictured herself standing there, dry, complacent, saying to the sodden figure, "What's the matter, Ogden?" She smiled sadly as she walked on.

Well, it had been a nice idea. She had assumed that any man with a Ph.D. and a flat stomach, a man who could make that inspiring speech to the town meeting, must be a lively and stimulating person, in tune with her own sensitivities, alive to the issues of the day. She had taken it for granted that he would not slam doors, although she had to grin at her own naïveté.

She had always placed professors on pedestals, but surely by now she must be old enough to know better. Professor Gibson, that sweet-syllabled orator who had taught her Romantic poetry in college, was said to have beaten his children with a razor strap when they failed to wash their hands before dinner. And Professor O'Flaherty. He of the beautiful smile and the musical accent, who taught moral philosophy every Monday and Wednesday at 10:30 A.M., had actually placed his hand on her thigh one morning after class, when he was discussing her essay topic with her. And *squeezed* it. She had never forgotten it, and henceforth it was as though her thigh were tainted. Squeeze anything else, she had often thought, later in life, but keep your hands off my right thigh. It had always puzzled Basil—and small wonder. "What on earth is so special about that leg?" he'd say, irritated, when she would cringe from his touch. And every time she saw that meek little wife of Professor O'Flaherty's downtown or at a concert she would actually feel again that outrageous pressure.

However, it now appeared to Mrs. Knickle that she was to spend the rest of her life without squeezing of any kind. As she walked through Centennial Gardens she watched the strolling couples and felt a wave of deep regret. Old age might change you on the outside. But inside you felt exactly the same as when you were young. She ached with envy of the young people around her. Mr. VanBuskirk had seemed such a perfect solution to her loneliness. She walked home so slowly that there could not possibly have been any cardiovascular benefit whatsoever.

But Mrs. Knickle was already switching her channel by the time she arrived home. She entered the house, closing the screen door carefully, quietly, behind her. She was tired. How lovely to be able to sit down before the soaps with a peanut butter sandwich, instead of having to prepare a complicated lunch for someone else. How nice to be able to indulge her interest in *The Young and the Restless* without worrying about the almost-certain disapproval of a higher mind—a mind fixed on galaxies.

"Hello, Jonas dear," she said to her canary, admiring his plumage and his voice. Observing the dustballs skittering across the floor, she thought aloud, "Go ahead. Skitter. I'm in no mood today to deal with you." Then she ate her sandwich, watched her program, and went to bed, sleeping soundly for exactly forty-five minutes.

When she awoke, the beautiful sunny day had deteriorated and dark clouds were gathering in the east and overhead. An intermittent plink-plink on the rain spouting told her what she could expect for the rest of the day. A few stray gulls flew across the sky swiftly, purposefully, without their usual lazy gyrations. A storm, she knew, was on its way. And a good one. "There will be wind and a lot of rain," she said. "Which calls for a fire in the grate and a book on the sofa." She changed into her purple housecoat, the one with the embroidered yoke and the covered buttons, gift of her youngest son on her most recent birthday. Then she lit the fire and settled herself on the sofa with an afghan, a glass of dry sherry, and one of Robertson Davies's novels.

"It's a sign," she said, contentedly. "It was meant to

be. The storm came in order to remind me of this fact."
She hugged her freedom close to herself and smiled quietly. That was at 2:30.

At 3:30, two logs and fifty-nine pages later, the doorbell rang. Mrs. Knickle left her comfortable nest on the sofa and placed her book, open and butter-side down, on the afghan. She could see through the window that the rain was descending in driving, gusting curtains of gray. She opened the front door.

It was Mr. VanBuskirk. Without umbrella or raincoat, he stood there, unbelievably wet, a measuring cup in his hand.

"I beg your pardon," he said. "I'm dripping all over your carpet," for she had gestured that he come in from the veranda. The wind was such that the rain reached right across into the front door. And it was cold. She closed the door and tried to bring her astonishment under control.

"It never occurred to me that one could get this wet, going just the distance of four houses," Mr. VanBuskirk said, water running into his eyes and dripping into his collar.

It crossed Mrs. Knickle's mind that anyone with an advanced knowledge of physics could have figured this out. "Here," she said briskly, suddenly all efficiency.

"Come in by the fire. Take off your shirt and wrap yourself in that afghan. I'll get one of Basil's old sweaters for you. Unless, of course, you want to get pneumonia and spoil the entire summer for yourself. Sit down on that wingback chair."

When she returned with Basil's sweater—a soft red cashmere that she could never bring herself to dispose of—Mr. VanBuskirk was sitting huddled in the chair, engulfed by the afghan.

"I think I'm getting your chair wet," he shivered. He reflected for a moment. Myra would not have liked that at all, and would have rushed to get newspapers or cushions to put under him.

"Don't talk nonsense," Mrs. Knickle said brusquely. "Here's a towel to dry yourself, and a sweater. Put it on while I'm making coffee. Would you like it laced with a little whisky to warm you up?"

Mr. VanBuskirk turned his amazing eyes upon her and said simply, "Oh my!"

She gave him ten minutes to recover his temperature and his dignity, and then returned with two steaming cups of Irish coffee and a plate of lemon-frosted carrot cake.

"Don't talk," she said. "Just eat. You'll feel better in a minute."

He did. He felt better almost immediately. His shaggy gray hair had been toweled vigorously and was already starting to dry. He smiled shyly above his whisky-coffee.

"I came to borrow some brown sugar," he said, his eyes avoiding hers. "I like it on my porridge. Oatmeal. I knew you had some. Because of Ogden, you know."

"Yes," she said. She did not say that it seemed an odd day to choose to collect it.

Mr. VanBuskirk looked up from his coffee. "I see you have a canary," he said. "As birds go, it's attractive. Although I feel that wild things should be free. However, it sings nicely. I don't think it would disturb a person who was reading." Then he added gloomily, "I keep a cat."

She absorbed this extraordinary paragraph. "Yes, I know," she said. "So do I."

"Yes? Oh. Well, well. It doesn't endanger the canary?"

"I have yet to see the cat that can climb a stainless steel rod. And the canary, as you so aptly pointed out, is not free."

"Yes. Yes, of course."

There was a silence that was not uncomfortable.

"I've read your book." He nodded toward the volume on the sofa. "I found the ending very contrived."

Mrs. Knickle spoke carefully. "So far, I like it a lot," she said. "I'll assess the ending when I get there."

"Your cake," he said slowly—everything he did seemed to be slow—"is like an edible poem."

"Or perhaps like edible physics."

He chuckled. "More like physics. Because physics is beyond poetry, and better."

And then there followed a lively discussion, an out-and-out argument on poetry versus physics. She knew again that delicious sensation of mental tautness that she had almost forgotten. That lively reaching for the logical reply. That rallying of ideas, like an invigorating game of tennis. When they had finished their discussion, no opinions had changed. But it had been fun. It had been stimulating to feel that brisk turning of cerebral wheels.

At five o'clock, Mr. VanBuskirk rose slowly from the wingback chair. "I see the storm is over," he said. "I must be going. Supper, you know."

Mrs. Knickle resisted the temptation to ask him to share the remains of last night's casserole. She didn't want to proceed with undue haste. Besides, a gourmet cook doesn't want to make her début with a menu of leftovers.

"Oh!" she said suddenly, as he reached the door. "I forgot." She hurried back to the kitchen.

"Here," she said. "Your sugar. I'm getting so forgetful. And a bit of carrot cake for your supper."

Mr. VanBuskirk looked gratefully at Mrs. Knickle. He observed her crazy hairdo, the profusion of white curls. He admired her bright eyes. He marveled at her quick movements. He coughed slightly.

"Mrs. Knickle," he began. This was difficult for him. He could not draw on a lifetime of habit. "Mrs. Knickle, I would like to tell you that I like your . . . robe. A very lovely color. And becoming. And I thank you for your rescue mission."

He watched her. His compliment had pleased her. It was clear to him that this was so. The delight in her eyes was unmistakable. He sighed as he turned toward the porch. Poor Myra. It would have been so easy. He opened the screen door and slammed it behind him.

Mrs. Knickle scarcely heard the slamming of the door. She did not move out to the kitchen to preheat the oven. Instead, she went into the living room and sat down on a footstool, staring at the fire. She was a little bit sad. It was that remark about the purple housecoat that had done it. With one blow, he had deprived her of her freedom—acquired, relinquished, and freshly regained. She knew he would never speed up. Clearly there was slowness built right into his genes. That screen door would be slamming until she died. Two cats in one house argue over territory—just like two people. Jonas would be safe, but possibly too nervous to sing. Mr. VanBuskirk

193

was unlikely to be the type to dry dishes, either quickly or slowly.

Then she rose from the footstool and looked at herself in the mirror above the mantlepiece. She passed her right hand across the embroidered yoke of her housecoat and down the soft purple material of her left sleeve. She smiled to herself in the glass. "Becoming," she whispered.

"Nothing," she said aloud, as she went out to the kitchen to heat her tuna casserole, "is ever simple."

About the Author

BUDGE WILSON began writing for children at the age of fifty. Her book *The Leaving*, was an ALA Best Book for Young Adults, an ALA Notable Book, A *Horn Book* Fanfare selection, a *School Library Journal* Best Book of the Year, an ALA "75 Best Books for the last 25 Years," A Library of Congress 100 Noteworthy Book of the Year, and it received many other awards and prizes.

Her novels and stories have been translated into many languages. The most recently published, *The Dandelion Garden*, was hailed by *Publishers Weekly* in a starred review as "demonstrating a profound understanding of humanity"; and *School Library Journal* said in a starred review, "Not to be missed."

Budge Wilson is the mother of two daughters and lives with her husband, Alan, and their cat in a fishing village near Hubbards, Nova Scotia.